KIDNAPPED BY PIRATES

By

EVELYN GILL HILTON

BASED ON THE TRUE STORY OF CHARLES TILTON, WHO WAS CAPTURED FROM A WHALER AS A BOY BY JEAN LAFITTE'S PIRATES

*Illustrations by Evelyn Gill Hilton,
with some from Dover Co. & Lafitte Museum ,
Huntsville, TX. (www.texastrailsbooks.com)"*

Order this book online at www.trafford.com
or email orders@trafford.com

Most Trafford titles are also available at major online book retailers.

Printed in Victoria, BC, Canada.

ISBN: 978-1-4269-2017-2 (sc)
ISBN: 978-1-4269-2018-9 (hc)

Library of Congress Control Number: 2009940293

*Our mission is to efficiently provide the world's finest, most comprehensive book publishing
service, enabling every author to experience success. To find out how to publish your book, your
way, and have it available worldwide, visit us online at www.trafford.com*

Trafford rev. 3/29/2010

 www.trafford.com

North America & international
toll-free: 1 888 232 4444 (USA & Canada)
phone: 250 383 6864 ♦ fax: 812 355 4082

Outline

DEDICATION

I dedicate this book to my wonderful husband, Bob, who helped me with research and stood by with great patience while I wrote. Thank you for helping me in my quest to know my ancestors. I love you.

Evelyn

And In Memory Of

My Mother, Charlene Morgan Gill, who, though she grew up poor, was rich in her love of her family and God's beautiful earth. She taught me to appreciate and research our ancestors and she passed her passion for the beach and the sea on to me.

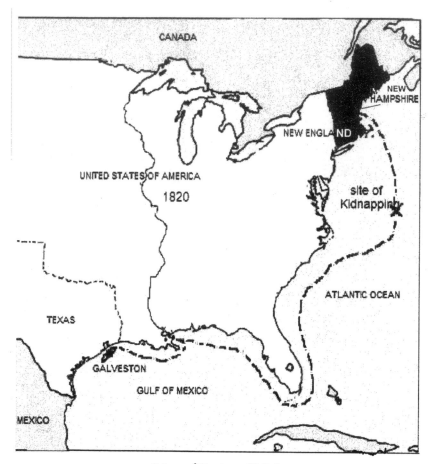

Map of Eastern U.S.A.

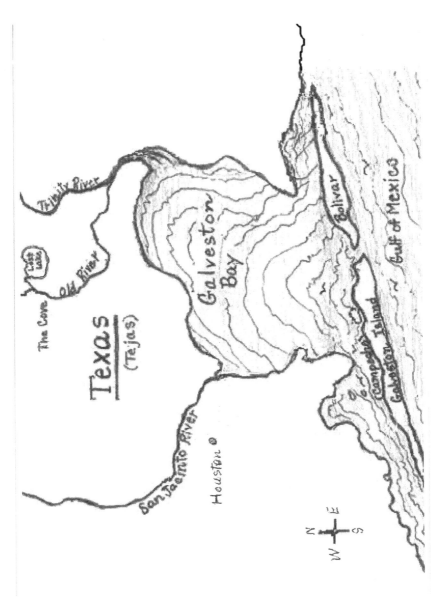

Texas Coastal Map 1800s

Chapter 1:

The Beginning

Summer, 1814~~Somewhere Off the Eastern Seaboard of America

A prisoner, fourteen year-old Charles Tilton leaned heavily against the railing of the sleek, teak wood, pirate schooner watching the fearful sight on the deck of the *Evening Star*, the big whaler where he worked. Some of the wooden barrels of gunpowder he had helped carry up from the hold to the deck of the whaler were exploding. Men shouted and flintlock pistols fired. He could see the metallic glint of the short cutlasses and hear the clash of the longer swords amidst the yells. Fires blazed, creating billowing smoke and confusion everywhere as the sailors engaged in life or death duels with the bloodthirsty pirates.

If it weren't for the iron ball and chain the pirates had attached to his ankle, Charles would gladly jump over the side of the schooner and swim to his ship. He would climb up the rope jack ladder, hanging on the side of the *Evening Star*, and fight with the other whalers in their efforts to fend off the cutthroats. He knew he could be killed along with other innocent sailors but, oh, what a fight he would put up against these evil heathens! His knuckles turned white as he gripped the rail in anger.

Charles would be a good, brave soldier like is father. In his shock, his mind escaped back to the battles his father, Green Tilton, had fought in the American Revolution, stories told to him and his sisters many times over the years.

America, a New Country & a New Home

Charles' father, Green Tilton, and his mother, Judith Favor, who was a Quaker, had both come to America from England. As a young man, Green joined the American Revolution and fought with George Washington to help win America's freedom from England in 1776.

After the war, Green apprenticed for the only job he had ever known—whaling. It was dangerous work, just as his father before him had done in England, but the love of the sea had always run in the Tilton men's blood. Green signed on with the huge wooden sailing Ship, the *Evening Star*, that sailed out twice a year from New Hampton, New Hampshire, for four-month whaling trips on the Atlantic Ocean.

Green and Judith were happily married and he built them a home not far from the wharves in the seacoast town. He joined the Friends Church but did not use the Quaker speech of "thee and thou," like Judith, a Quaker since birth. In October of 1799, Charles Nathan Tilton, was born, the fourth of seven children and the first boy after three girls. He was a handsome lad who looked much like his father, with coal-black hair, fair skin and a determined chin. But, like his mother, he had eyes "as green and bright as the noontime sea," as she sometimes told him.

Judith schooled Charles, along with his three older sisters and younger siblings, at home. They learned to read and write from the Bible and to cipher numbers using pieces of charcoal on boards.

Young Charles, Mother, Brothers and Sisters

Charles often daydreamed about going to sea and Mother Judith would scold him. "Charles, thee is a smart lad. Thee must study and learn to show thyself approved!" Her usual gentle speech would take on a stern tone and Charles could see a strong glint of determination in her bright green eyes.

"Yes, Mother, I am sorry," he would answer as he shook his head to bring his thoughts back to his lessons.

During all his early years the smart, slim boy trailed behind his father always asking about ships and whaling, for he loved the ocean almost as much as his father and grandfather did. Green had no doubt in his mind that his young son, Charles, would one day go to sea. If he had only known what a terrible, dangerous ocean journey Charles was destined to face, he would have forbidden his son to ever step foot on a ship.

Chapter 2:

Charles goes A'Whaling~~Spring, 1814

One day, Charles' father walked the six blocks from their home to his ship for some papers and he took the boy along. Sailors were climbing down and hanging by ropes they had draped over the side of the ship to scrape its wooden hull. They waved to Charles and he waved back.

"Look, Father! What are they doing?"

Green answered, "Son, they are scraping barnacles off the ship."

"Why are they doing that?" the curious boy asked.

"Those little shell-like animals keep the ship from going fast so the sailors scrape down the boat whenever we come into port," his father replied, smiling at his interest.

"I wish I could help them and I wish I could go a'whaling with you this year, Father! Am I old enough yet?" This and every other year, young Charles would beg his father.

But every year the answer would be the same. "Lad, I need you to stay here, finish your schooling and take care of your mother, sisters and wee brothers."

Charles hung his head in disappointment and a lock of black hair fell over his eyes. "Yes sir," he said obediently, until the next year.

The years went by and, when Charles was fourteen years old, he asked again. "Father, do you think I am old enough to go a'whaling this season?" He straightened his slim frame and held his shoulders back to try and appear larger. He was now a handsome youth. Green gazed down at his tall, black-haired son with chiseled features that included a straight nose and a square chin like his own.

With a smile flickering around his mouth, Green finally said, "I reckon this year you are old enough to find out what sort of work you want for your livelihood. Aye son, you can go a'whaling with me but remember, 'tis hard work and no play. And you will need to continue your schooling when we are in port."

Charles' could hardly believe his ears. "Oh, thank you, Father, I will work hard and make you proud!" His stunning green eyes sparkled and his fair cheeks flushed with excitement.

His father continued, "I have already inquired of my friend, James Thatcher, the Captain of the *Evening Star*. He is an excellent captain and she's a fine, sturdy ship. He is willing to let you come along with me as an apprentice without pay this time. If you do well, then you can go out as a paid sailor on our next trip."

Charles understood well about working free. It was a good way to learn a trade or pay off a debt. His mother, Judith, had worked as an indentured servant for five years for a New Hampton family who had paid for her passage to America. Although Charles was thrilled about his new job, his mother was not happy about her young son going to sea. Since her three older children were girls, this would be her first child to go a'whaling in his father and grandfather's footsteps.

"Thee does not know how dangerous a job this be, son. I think thee too young to go." She shook her head tearfully as she spoke. Charles usually loved to listen to her soft, lilting voice, but now he turned his head in an effort to ignore it. After Father assured her many times that Charles would be under the watchful eyes of Captain Thatcher and himself, she finally begrudgingly agreed.

Charles' younger brothers and sister, Ethan, Molly, Jonah and baby Matthew, watched in awe as he began packing his duffel bag with warm clothes. He would later discover the jar of sweet apple butter his mother had tucked into the bottom of the bag.

"Don't let a shark bite thee," four year-old Jonah advised soberly, his eyes big and round with apprehension.

"Are you afraid you might slip and fall overboard?" Ethan, who was three years younger than Charles, asked as a trace of fear rose in his voice.

"Of course not! When I am on deck I shall be careful and I will stay away from the railing in rough seas," Charles laughingly assured him, promising himself that he would be extra cautious. The thought of falling into the cold, heaving sea was not a pretty one.

A week before the sailing, Father went up on the roof of their house to patch a leak. The wood shingles were wet and, on his way down, he slipped and tumbled headlong onto the ground. He knew at once that his arm was broken and he would not be able to go to sea this season. While Mother splinted and bandaged the arm, Father bemoaned his misfortune because he knew he would lose four months' good wages.

"No, Father," Charles interrupted. "I will go in your stead and the Captain will pay me half-wages." It was a long-standing custom for another fit man in the family to go a'whaling in the place of a hurt whaler at half wages. This kept the whaler from losing all of his pay and way of supporting his family.

"No, son. You don't have any experience and you are only fourteen. I can not allow you to do that."

"Father," Charles pleaded. "I am the same age as you were when you first went a'whaling and you were alone. Besides I know Captain Thatcher and some of the sailors. They will watch over me and I will be extra careful."

Green looked sadly at his wife and finally he slowly nodded in agreement. There was simply no other choice.

Early on the morning of the sailing, Charles sat down, along with the rest of the family, to pray and eat breakfast. Miriam, his oldest sister, served him an extra spoonful of mother's good, hot porridge. Sarah gave him her portion of precious honey for his cereal while Ruth sliced the thick bread and cheese for him. His mother smiled as he thanked his sisters and gobbled up the good food. A little later, he hoisted his stuffed duffel bag over his shoulder and walked with his family through the thick New England coastal fog down to the ship dock.

While they stood on the wharf with the other sailors' families, Mother said tearfully, "I'll keep a lamp in the window for thee, my darlin' son." She spoke of the custom of burning a light in an ocean-facing window sill to guide the whaler home from the sea. Charles gently kissed her wet cheek and she pulled a necklace from her pocket. "I have kept this for many years but it now belongs to you. 'Twas me own dear grandmother's. 'Tis a reminder that God will keep ye safe if ye trust in Him, no doubt." He tenderly fingered the necklace as she put it around his neck, then thanked her and hugged his brothers and sisters.

When he came to Miriam, his oldest sister, she slipped a small silver ring into his hand. "This is the ring that Grandmother Tilton sent to me from England. May it will help keep you safe." Charles put it on, smiled and gave her a long hug. Then, for the first time in his life, he shook hands with his father. Green looked at the smaller, slender hand in his own large, callused one and swallowed heavily.

"Be careful, son. Do not complain and watch your footing on deck for it is often slick with sea spray." Father's voice cracked as he spoke gruffly. Then he suddenly threw his good arm tightly around his oldest son and bid him farewell.

"Fare thee well and God speed thee home to us, Charles." His mother repeated the familiar seaman's farewell and waved while he walked up the narrow gangplank and onto the huge, wooden whaling ship.

NewEngland Whaler in Harbor

Standing at the stern of the ship with the other crew members, Charles pulled himself up as tall as he could and shouted confidently to his family, "Don't worry, I'll be back in only four months!"

Charles could hear them calling, along with the other families, "God speed and safe return!" The anchor chain was pulled up and the canvas sails were raised. The boy tasted the salty tang of the sea on his lips and his heart raced with excitement.

Then the *Evening Star* began to slowly move out of the New Hampton harbor. Suddenly, Charles felt a wave of loneliness sweep over him. He watched the white handkerchiefs his mother and sisters waved with a tinge of sadness until the heavy fog closed in and he could no longer see them. Only then did he realize that the salty taste on his mouth was from his tears.

The sad moment was soon broken by the captain calling the men to order. The sailors quickly lined up to listen to his words. "Welcome back for another whaling season, men."

The stout captain stood tall and proud before the sixteen-man crew. Although his voice boomed, Charles could see friendliness in his weathered, bearded face.

"Aye, aye, Captain," the men responded.

Evelyn Gill Hilton

"We have an apprentice on board this trip. You all know his father, Green Tilton, a good and respected whaler who has sailed with us for many years." The captain pointed to Charles. "His son, Charles, here is standing in for him this season for half-wages, so we will help him learn the ropes. I'm assigning him to the galley to work for Corky."

"Aye, Captain," a huge man, responded hardily.

Someone shouted, "Is there room in the ship's kitchen for both Corky and the lad?"

Friendly laughter radiated among the men but the loudest came from the heavy, jolly cook, himself. The boy glanced at Corky and was greeted with a friendly wink and a grin. Charles decided at once that he liked all of these whalers, especially Corky.

"Watch it, Williams, or you may find a fish head in yer stew this eve!" Another hardy laugh resounded from the men as Corky chuckled, glancing at Charles. Such was the jovial banter among the crew daily on the *Evening Star* and Charles happily participated.

Although he forgot his family for the moment, the image of them waving and the sound of their parting words would remain in Charles' mind and heart much longer than he could possibly imagine. It would be many years before he saw his loved ones again. The course of his new life was now set in motion and, like the whaler that was slicing through the cold, dark ocean waters, it could carry him seaward onto the vast Atlantic and on a terrifying but adventurous path. Even if angels had told the boy, he would not have believed what lay ahead for him.

Evening Star Whalers Going After a Whale

Chapter 3:

In Search of the Great Humpbacks

The billowing, white sails of the *Evening Star* filled with the western, seaward wind that always blew off the land in the early morning. The ship sailed out of the harbor and into the enormous Atlantic Ocean. The sailors were going out in search of the great Humpback Whales that were plentiful in the cold, deep waters off the eastern coast of North America. In the 1800s, there was no electricity for light, so people depended almost totally on whale blubber (or whale fat) for lamp oil, candles, cooking oil, and the nutritious whale meat that was used for food.

Charles was thrilled to be on his first trip on a ship. Like the other sailors, he was given a hemp rope hammock to sleep in and told to hang it near the others below deck wherever he could find a place. Every morning each sailor rolled up his hammock with his possessions inside it and put the bundle against the wall so the room could be used for work during the day.

The captain of the ship had assigned Charles to the galley to work under the watchful eye of Corky because he thought it would be the safest place for a young man's first voyage. Charles appreciated that the portly, lighthearted man treated him like an equal rather than a child. This encouraged Charles greatly and almost made him forget his homesickness and his nagging seasickness. Corky gave him the daily task of bringing up boxes of grub from the ship's hold below to the galley, where they cooked the meals.

"You will save my knees," Corky said grinning. "It's hard going up and down the stair cases with these old joints."

"It is no problem, sir. I'm glad to be of help," Charles replied eagerly with a grin.

He was also given the job of washing dirty pots when Corky finished with them and of clearing the tables after the sailors ate. He did not mind these tasks and did them with a cheerfulness that caused Corky to brag to Captain Thatcher about him.

"Charles, lad, you're doing a good job," Corky remarked to the boy one day.

"Thank you, sir," Charles replied grinning. He felt proud that he had pleased Corky and sat a heavy box of salted pork down on the counter.

Corky took the pieces of meat out and rinsed them in water to wash off the preserving salt that kept the meat from spoiling. Then he dropped the pork into a big pot of boiling water and added dried beans from a sack in the corner. Charles was relieved to see that the ship stove had a railing around it to keep the pots from flying off during rough seas.

"Go ahead and shell this sack of corn and then grind the kernels in this grinder for cornbread, lad. That and beans will do us for sup tonight," he grunted. "Later, I might let you mix up some of that hasty puddin' with syrup that you tell me your mom taught you to make."

"Yes, sir!" Charles replied eagerly, proud to be able to show Corky a new dish. He took several ears of corn out of the sack and began rubbing the kernels off the corn cobs with his thumbs and palms. As he dropped the dry, yellow kernels into the pan, he realized that he liked this work in the galley. The warm smells reminded him of his mother's kitchen, though not quite as desirable.

His thoughts were interrupted by a call from the sailor on watch in the crow's nest. "Humpback Whale! Thar she blows!" Charles knew he was referring to the water a whale spouts through the hole on top of its head. His ears perked up and his eyes widened in the excitement.

"Shiver me timbers! He's spotted our first whale!" Corky boomed. He knew that Charles would like to see the men bring in the humpback. "Go on," he told boy, gesturing toward the staircase that led up to the deck.

Charles threw off his apron, pulled on his jacket and bounded up the stairs three at a time. He didn't mind the cold salt spray that splashed in his face and leaned carelessly over the ship's wooden rail to watch the action.

Sailors Going After a Whale

Just when a rowboat, filled with sailors, was lowered into the sea, a small fish near the ship broke the water's surface and caught the boy's eye. He watched intently while it plopped back down into a school of hundreds more fish and they all sped away like little silver bullets. Charles was so caught up in watching the fish that he didn't notice how far he was hanging over the side. Suddenly, the ship rolled into a wave and he lost his grip on the railing.

"Whoa, boy! Are ya thinking of goin fer a swim with the fishes?" An old sailor grabbed Charles' arm just as he was loosing his balance. "Better get yer sea legs and yer wits about ya!"

"No, sir—I mean, yes sir—I mean thank you, sir." Charles' cheeks turned bright red. He was frightened and embarrassed at his foolishness.

The sailor beamed and his friendly grin revealed two missing teeth in front. "Just watch your step, lad. I lost these long ago from being careless." He extended a bony hand toward his missing teeth then stretched it out toward Charles. "I'm Lester."

Charles shyly shook hands with the skinny sailor and introduced himself. He breathed a heavy sigh of relief and backed away from the railing. Remembering his father's warning, he promised himself that he would be more careful from now on. He didn't want to experience the humiliation of being pulled out of the cold sea.

Then Charles began watching the rowboat and sailors. When their boat came within throwing distance of the whale, two men stood up with long spears tied to rope coils. They heaved the spears and harpooned the animal, killing it. Soon the sailors rowed back to the ship dragging the whale behind the boat. Ropes were tied around the floating carcass and it was heaved up onto the deck. Even Corky and Charles were called on to help with the heavy task now at hand.

The sailors started processing the meat right away. The Whale fat, or blubber, was boiled down for oil in a big, covered, iron pot that was bolted onto a metal floor in the middle of the ship's deck. The thick metal kept the ship's wood deck beneath it safe from the fire. The blubber melted when it was heated and turned to oil in the vat. Then it was carefully poured into wooden barrels and stored to be sold in port and later made into precious candles and lamp oil. The whale meat was salted down, also be sold back in port. Even the bones would be used for needles and other important household items.

Charles had heard his father tell about whaling but could never quite understand until he saw it for himself. He felt sorry for the whale but reminded himself that this was a necessary job that helped people have food and lamp light. He realized that he was excited and proud to be a whaler like his father and grandfather and great grandfather.

Chapter 4:

Ahoy, Skull 'n Crossbones!

For the next month into the *Evening Star's* voyage, the crew scouted for and got two more whales. Charles learned to raise and trim, or lower, the canvas sails and to mend them, using whale bone needles. He was never quite sure where they were in latitude or longitude, only that they were somewhere off the northeastern coast of America. A light breeze filled out the sails as the whaler glided through the cold, deep water. He glanced contentedly at the cloudless, blue sky while scrubbing the deck along with some of the other sailors. He had "gotten his sea legs," become used to the rocking ship and his seasickness had finally vanished.

Lester toted a bucket of seawater over to them and, chuckling softly, he emptied it a little too near the boy. The cold water hit Charles' bare feet and, startled, he jumped up. "Yow!" He yelped.

He whirled around and saw his toothless old friend. "Look at ya! Jumped like a frog, ya did, lad!" The other sailors all burst out laughing, and Charles laughed too. The men were becoming like big brothers and uncles to Charles and they all liked him because of his willingness to work hard and his good humor. He didn't mind being the butt of their jokes and tricks because he knew that many were played on the rookies to keep away the boredom.

Suddenly, high up in the crow's nest on the main mast, the watcher shouted loudly, "Ship Ahoy!"

Sailor in Crows Nest

Captain Thatcher hastened to the deck railing and pulled the telescope out of his coat pocket. He noted aloud that it was a schooner, a sleek, narrow ship, flying an American flag. In these times, a strange ship on the high seas was always a concern because of treacherous pirates and the heavily-armed Spanish galleons.

"No need for alarm, men," the whaling captain called out and put the telescope back into his pocket. "Go back to work.

It's an American vessel!" Pirate ships almost never sailed this far north so Captain Thatcher did not suspect that evil buccaneers manned the schooner's wheel.

*****

Using a common trick, the scoundrels had fooled the captain by flying an American flag. The narrow, long schooner moved much faster than the bulky whaler and, as they came closer, the friendly flag would be lowered and the skull and crossbones flag was raised.

"Easy pickings!" the greedy pirate captain, Jay Rooster, cried confidently to his men. The whaler was just too good of a looting prize for him to pass up.

Pirates Sighting Prey

"But, Sir," his first mate, Jim Groggins, said fearfully. "Bos forbids us attacking American ships under penalty of death!"

"But Bos ain't here, is he? And I'll slit the throat of the one that tells 'em we are!" Rooster yelled. He gave the crew an evil snarl. A captain's word was, and is still, law on the ship.

Rooster snorted, "She sits low in the water with her barrels of whale oil. If we brings Bos prize booty what can be sold, he'll be glad. Besides who's to know what flag the ship flew if she's lying at the bottom of the sea with Davy Jones' Locker?" His evil mind was set on attacking the whaler and Groggins knew better than to argue with him. He had seen men lose their lives for disputing this vicious captain over far less.

*****

On the *Evening Star*, the men went back to their work. Another American ship was a welcome sight. But in a few minutes the sailor up in the crow's nest yelled, "Cap'n, take another look. They're raising the Jolly Roger!" The American flag had been lowered and a black skull and crossbones was now being hoisted to the top of the mast.

"Our worst fears are realized," Captain Thatcher muttered in horror as he looked through his telescope again.

He turned and yelled to the crew, "Pirate ship! Man your General Quarters now and bring up the barrels of gun powder and cannon balls!"

Indeed, this was a ship captain's worst nightmare. Captain Thatcher had never been attacked by the vicious marauders but had heard tales about them. They were skilled marksmen and even better with swords, rarely showing mercy to their prisoners.

"Cap'n, Can we outrun 'em?" One of the men asked frantically.

The captain shook his head sadly but quickly. "No, they're sailing a schooner. Our ship is too big and heavy to outrun that slim boat. We will have to stand and fight the riffraff!" He knew that his ship was out-gunned and out-manned.

Charles stepped up. "Captain, I'll fight the scum, too. Give me a pistol!" He was eager to help.

"No, Charles." The captain shook his head firmly. "I promised your father that I would keep you safe. You are too young to face cutthroats, should they come aboard. You can help the men bring cannon balls up on deck, then hide yourself well below."

Captain Thatcher pointed to the men bringing up the small barrels of gunpowder and cannon balls from the powder room. Canvas covers were quickly untied and ripped off the cannons and weapons were handed out to every man as they flew into action.

Although disappointed, the boy obeyed and helped carry up cannon balls. As the pirate ship drew closer, he was then ordered to get below. He glanced back toward the oncoming schooner and could now see the black flag it was flying.

Corky came rushing up the staircase past him with his gun. "Tarnation lad, get below and hide! "Make tracks now!"

The schooner was fast closing the gap between the two ships. Every whaler steeled himself for a bitter life or death fight with the evil cutthroats.

Ship Captain Sights Pirates

Charles' hand went to the little gold cross around his neck and he said a quick prayer as his mother has taught him to do in time of trouble. He scampered down the stairs like a rabbit running for its life.

Chapter 5:

Battling the Pirates

The New England whaler's captain, William Thatcher, rubbed his chin in worry and anxiously yelled, "Wait for my order to fire, mates! I want those slimy scumbags close enough for our cannon balls to hit them."

He had only a total of four cannons, two on each side of the whaler, since it was not a fighting ship but he knew the pirate schooner was extremely well armed. His sailors had loaded their pistols, placed cannon balls into the cannons and loaded the firing pins with gunpowder. Now the men stood at attention, ready to light the fuses. Cannon balls barrels of gun powder had been brought up from the hold to the deck and now the whalers awaited Captain Thatcher's order to fire. He watched the sleek schooner cut through the waves, until it came within firing range.

In a loud voice, the captain suddenly cried out, "Fire!"

The cannon masters took careful aim at their fast-moving target and lit the fuses. It only took several seconds for the fuses to burn down into the cannon chambers and ignite the small sacks of gunpowder behind the cannon balls. The gunpowder exploded with loud blasts and propelled the iron balls out through the air and toward the pirates' schooner.

✶✶✶✶✶

Rooster, the schooner's captain, was watching Captain Thatcher through his telescope and anticipated this action. As soon as the captain shouted the order and waved his arm, Rooster spun the wheel, steering the schooner into a swerve. This often-used tactic gave the pirates just enough time to set in motion a zigzag course of dodging and pursuing. More cannon balls were fired, but most of them missed the veering schooner. The two that hit did only slight damage. Since the whaler was much slower due to its size and weight, the pirates began to close in. Then the cunning pirate captain ordered several well placed cannon shots. One of them pierced the whaler's hull at sea level and caused the *Evening Star* to begin taking on water.

Cannon fire continued between the two ships but very soon the pirates pulled alongside the whaler. The evil Rooster, enraged that the whaler's captain had dared to fire on his schooner, lifted his sword high and gave the order to board.

"Hook the whaler and board 'er, mates!" he shouted. Long ropes with large boarding hooks were thrown over the whaler's railing and then a gangplank was heaved up from the schooner and secured between the two ships. Within minutes the fierce pirates, holding knives between their teeth and armed with muskets and short swords called cutlasses, swarmed aboard the whaler. With bloodcurdling screams and shouting oaths, the pirates began fighting in hand-to-hand combat with the sailors.

Men shouted while pistols fired and barrels of gunpowder exploded. For a while, it seemed like the whalers might actually drive the pirates off their ship, but they were vastly outnumbered. Suddenly the tide turned when the vicious Groggins, Rooster's first mate, managed to slip up on Captain Thatcher and grab him from behind. Rooster saw his opportunity, ran over and pressed his cutlass against the captain's throat. "Order yer men to put down their arms and we'll let them live!" Rooster snarled cruelly at his captive.

Pirates Attack the Crew of the Evening Star

In order to save the lives of his crew members, the Captain Thatcher had no choice but to surrender. He shouted to his crew to put down their arms and they reluctantly obeyed. With a murderous yell, the pirates descended into the ship's hold where the cargo was stored and where Charles had been ordered to hide. Now the whalers of the *Evening Star* were completely at the mercy of Rooster and Groggins and their scoundrels.

*****

Evening Star Whaler Begins to Sink

Charles heard the pirates as they scrambled down the stairs and into the hold and he held his breath in horror. It wasn't long before they discovered him hiding under a box behind barrels of whale oil. They pushed Charles up to the deck although he kicked and fought back with all his strength.

"Quit squirming, ya minnow, or we'll feed ya to the sharks!" One of the pirates cuffed his ear hard and yelled at him. They ignored Captain Thatcher's pleas to unhand the boy, having already noticed his silver ring and the gold cross hanging from his neck. Charles realized that because of his new clothes and shoes and his jewelry, the marauders would think he was well off and that his family might pay handsomely for him.

"No," Groggins shouted. "We'll take him hostage. His parents might pay fine ransom for him." Groggins shrieked with pain when the boy kicked him hard as he was being dragged across the gangplank to the schooner.

"Hold this young landlubber for ransom. It's easy to see he ain't no whaler. Might be a passenger with them new clothes 'n he might be worth a pretty penny," Groggins slapped Charles and growled the order to a dark-skinned pirate named Stubby. The ugly pirate grunted, eyeing Charles' clothes and shoes carefully and he fingered the small gold cross.

"You and Hong Kong watch 'em—he's slippery as a' eel!" Groggins yelled limping back over the gangplank to the whaler.

"Dis hold ya, shrimp. Jes' try jump ship with des irons on. You sink like rock!" A skinny Chinese pirate laughed cruelly when he clamped a ball and chain onto the boy's ankle. Frightened as he was, Charles could not help but notice the long, black pigtail hanging out beneath Hong Kong's headscarf and three missing fingers on Stubby's hand.

The main sail of the whaler had begun burning during the horrific battle and now the smaller mast and other sails had caught on fire, a death knell for any ship. The pirates hurriedly transported crates of food and rolled barrels of whale oil over the gangplank from the *Evening Star* onto the *Black Jack*. As the flaming whaler slowly began to sink beneath the waves, Charles' heart and spirit also sank.

Rooster ordered the rowboats to be dropped into the water and the whalers who were still alive be thrown into the sea. As the men swam to the boats, he leaned over the railing and bellowed, "Now row back to America, you mangy sea dogs!" Loud jeers went up among the pirates.

"No, give them some water!" Charles cried out. Suddenly, Stubby's huge fingerless fist collided with his jaw and an intense pain rushed through his head. Then darkness blanketed him and he sank to the deck.

A bucket of cold seawater was soon thrown on the boy, shocking him awake. The pirate called Hong Kong was standing over him snarling. "Now you learn manners. No yell at Cap'n, you pip-squeak maggot!" He turned and walked away, his dirty, black pigtail swinging behind him.

Charles struggled up and leaned against the schooner's railing. His knuckles tightened white on the bar in fury and despair. Forgetting about the pain in his jaw, he squinted to see if Captain Thatcher, Corky and Lester were among those in the rowboats. At last, he spotted Corky and the captain rowing and thought he recognized Lester in one of the other boats. For the moment he felt relieved and hoped a passing ship would pick them up, but knew it was very unlikely.

"God speed you all," he whispered.

Charles Now a Prisoner on Pirate Schooner

Chapter 6:

Captured Alone

Now a prisoner, fourteen year-old Charles Tilton stood on the deck of the pirate ship watching the whalers in the small boats rowing into the distance. At last, they vanished into the horizon like ghosts. Charles wished he could have fought with the sailors when these evil pirates had attacked them. If the leg irons hadn't prevented him from escaping, he could have helped defend the ship. He knew that he might have died, but oh, what a fight he would have put up against these wicked heathens! Now he wished that he could dive into the ocean and swim after the rowboats and his friends, though there was little chance of them being saved.

Just then, Charles heard Stubby growling. "Get below, fish bait!" Then he felt himself being shoved down the staircase into the hold. Tumbling head over ball and chain down the stairs, he landed at the bottom with a thud, hitting his head. He yelled in anger more than in pain. Meanwhile, pirates stood looking down into the hold, gloating and laughing at their prisoner.

"Is rascal still 'live?" Hong Kong squealed.

"He better be!" Stubby sneered. "Bos'll want the high ransom he's gonna bring."

Bos? Charles wondered. *Who is this boss?* Then he passed out.

Before there was a chance of being discovered by another vessel, the pirates checked the ship compass and set sail south to their headquarters in the Gulf of Mexico and the swamps near New Orleans. By the time Charles woke up, the pirate ship had traveled over forty knots away from the scene of the crime. As the only prisoner, the boy now had plenty of time to ponder the series of events that had brought him here and to think about his forthcoming fate. Homesick and frightened, he could not help but cry himself to sleep at night but, little by little, he stopped crying, knowing that his death would be too terrible a blow to his parents, and determined to make a plan of escape. He vowed to himself to live through this horror and to return home one day.

Young Charles loathed the schooner's vicious captain, cruel, red-haired Jay Rooster, who most likely had gotten his name from his bright red beard and strutting walk resembling that of a proud rooster. He never seemed to speak but only bellowed orders. Charles felt the same intense dislike for Rooster's first mate, Jim Groggins, a sly fox of a man who had one wicked, beady, black eye. The place where the other eye should have been was covered with a dirty black patch. He also had a scar that ran from the lower edge of it down to a mouth that sported an ugly, sneering grin most of the time.

"'Ear's yer vittles, yer majesty," Stubby taunted, eying Charles' good leather shoes as he kicked the boy and put a tray of food down beside him. Charles kept his mouth shut and his eyes down, knowing that would be what his father would tell him to do in order to save his life.

He sat on the floor to eat, since the ball and chain kept him from moving around easily. Every day he was given the same fare as the pirates had to eat: hard tack, a kind of hard biscuit, jerky, beans or some of the oatmeal they had stolen from the *Evening Star*, sometimes a fresh-cooked fish, a lime, or an occasional egg called "cackle fruit," from the hens kept in cages on board.

He had to pound the hard tack on the floor to remove the little weevils that were crawling in it. The food was certainly worse than what the whalers had, but Charles ate it because he knew he needed to keep up his strength.

One night, a wind came up and it wasn't long before thunder roared and lightening flashed. The storm became worse by the minute, heaving the waters this way and that. The schooner swayed back and forth on the big waves perilously. The bow of the schooner would rise to the top of a big crest and then slide down the backside of the foamy wave. As quickly as the ship righted itself, another wave would rise up. Cold seawater splashed over the deck and ran down into the hold, soaking Charles. He began to fear that he might be lost along with all the others and the ship as well.

He could hear Rooster and Groggins yelling for the sails to be rolled in so they wouldn't tear apart. "Batten down the hatches! Trim the sails, ya dirty sea dogs!" They shouted along with many oaths. Afraid as the men were of climbing the masts in a lightning storm, they were more afraid of their captain and first mate, so they shimmied up the tall poles and lowered the sails.

HongKong, Evil Pirate

Hong Kong was sent down to unlock the irons on the prisoner. In a quivering voice, he declared, "It is tsunami (the Chinese word for hurricane). We soon die!" Thinking that he meant "hurricane" did nothing to increase Charles' courage but he could hardly keep from laughing at the mean Chinaman, who was standing there quaking in his filthy boots. Suddenly a blinding flash of lightning hit the ship, burst through the hold's only porthole window and lit up the dark storage room as bright as day.

"Yips! Help!" Hong Kong screamed, jumped and flew back up the stairs to the deck.

"Wait! Unlock my leg iron!" Charles called but no one heard. He was all alone.

Water from the huge waves washing over the deck and from a new crack in the ship's side began to run into the hold. It wasn't long before the heavy Barrels of whale oil stored there started sliding back and forth. Dragging his ball and chain, Charles frantically dodged this way and that as they shifted and rolled. He was afraid that eventually one would knock him down and roll over him. If he became pinned under it, he knew he would drown.

The pirates are too busy saving themselves to come down here and release me, he thought in alarm. *What would Father do?* Charles knew he must calm down and think of a way to save himself.

Just then, a huge square crate with ropes tied around it skidded by the boy and gave him an idea. Charles waited until it came back by him and then, with all his might, he hoisted the ball and chain up on top of the crate and then pulled himself up by holding on to the ropes. For the rest of the night, the vessel dipped and pitched and dipped again. He lay on the crate, arms secured under the ropes and hands clutching the sides as the box slid to and fro' in the dark. Though wet, cold and tired beyond belief, he dared not shut his eyes for fear of falling asleep. His muscles ached but he prayed and sang and held on.

At last, morning came and the storm moved on. Hong Kong crept down, unlocked the chain around his ankle and ordered him up on deck. Exhausted, the boy crawled up the staircase and fell down on the deck. The warm sun soon dried Charles and the other men out and the ship continued on its way. Lying in the sunshine, he thought about his friends in the rowboats and wondered if the storm had overtaken them. He hoped not.

Charles felt a deep loathing for Rooster and Groggins, knowing that the pirate crew couldn't be blamed for the attack on the whaler as much as those two evil men. Pirate ships and whaling ships were run much the same as military ships, with the captain and first mate in complete control and their decisions regarded as law. Any member of the crew who dared to question them was considered a mutineer and met a swift death.

He also knew that his family had barely scrapped together the money to buy his new clothes and shoes and did not have money to pay a ransom, so he assumed that his own life might soon come to an end unless he could find a way to get away.

It wasn't long until Hong Kong came and pushed him back down into his dark hole. In his wildest dreams, Charles Tilton could never have imagined what the next chapter of his life would bring.

Raising the Skull and Crossbones

Chapter 7:

Spanish Galleon!

*I*n the afternoon, Charles' irons were again unlocked and he was brought up to the deck to gut and clean a mess of fish for the captain's supper. The ship's lookout suddenly spotted another vessel in the distance near the mainland. Checking through his telescope, Groggins saw that it was a Spanish galleon. He gave a whoop and ran to report what he had sited to Rooster. Soon, they were sailing toward the ship.

The King and Queen of Spain, a country in Europe, had claimed the newly-discovered land, now known as Mexico, and named it *New Spain*. They sent conquistadors to this new land and conquered it in the name of the King and Queen of Spain. Although explorers from Spain and the other European countries that explored and claimed land in the *New World*, or North and South America, did so under the guise of converting its people to Christianity, their ventures were mainly made for gold and glory for themselves and their countries. Many thousands of pounds of beautiful gems, gold and silver were mined in Mexico by the enslaved Indians under watchful eyes of armed Spanish soldiers.

Spain sent hundreds of galleons across the Atlantic Ocean to their territories to bring the riches home to the king and queen. Although the galleons traveled in large fleets of fifty to a hundred ships for safety, sometimes a heavily-loaded ship got separated from the others. It then quickly became "ripe pickin's" for the greedy pirates.

This heavily-loaded ship had somehow gotten separated from the others during the stormy night. The rich prize, there for the taking, was alone with her bow stuck on a sand bar. The stern sat low in the water, telling Rooster and Groggins that the ship was filled to the hilt with gold, silver, and gems from Mexico.

"The storm has beached 'er like a whale at low tide. This be our lucky day, mates!" Rooster thundered.

"Raise the Jolly Roger!" First Mate Groggins roared.

Charles saw the dreaded scull and crossbones being hoisted up the mast and heard the pirates cheering. He remembered when Rooster had attacked the whaler and his friends.

The schooner sailed close to the galleon and cannons from both ships boomed. A cannon ball hit the deck of the schooner, crashing through the wooden planks and into the hold where Charles was chained. Another one pierced the hull of the pirate schooner above the waterline. But the buccaneers gave as "good as they got"! Since most of the cannons were mounted on the sides of the galleon and the ship could not move, the Spaniards were at a grave disadvantage. It was just a matter of time before the heavy frigate sat crippled in the water with its sails in rags. The captain raised the white flag of surrender since there was no way of escape.

Ready for a fight, Rooster and his men soon threw down the gangplank and bounded onto the ship. The Spanish sailors and their attackers pulled out pistols and cutlasses and a bloody battle broke out. It wasn't long, however, before the pirates won.

"Pick 'em clean!" The evil Rooster barked. He grabbed the captain by his jacket and pointed his pistol to the man's head. "Where's the gold and silver?"

The captain didn't argue, but pointed toward the hold where the chests were stored. The pirates scrambled down the steps and found many crates of treasure, which they forced the Spaniards to haul over to the schooner.

"Cap'n," cried one of Rooster's men. "Look 'er what we found hid under the Spanish cap'n's own writin' table!" He dragged the largest chest with a gleaming metal lock up the staircase and set it in front of Rooster. "Want me to open it, sir?"

"No, we'll open this prize later." Rooster strutted over to the large chest and then eyed the captain of the galleon. The pirate laughed out loud. "It seems the cat has been caught with the mouse, eh, Captain?" He sneered. "So, ya have yer own private booty from Mexico!"

The captain's face was now scarlet and lined with fear. "No, no, I was only keeping it safe from thieving hands," blubbered the man, realizing he had indeed been caught hoarding treasure for himself. Stealing from shipmates was considered the lowest form of thievery among pirates.

Rooster sneered at the captain. "Ya was planning to keep this 'ere treasure fer yerself alone. Gimme the key!" The captain fumbled in his pockets and handed the large key to Rooster.

"Here is yer just reward, you swarthy scoundrel. Rooster shouted, "Shoot him, Groggins!" The first mate instantly raised his pistol and fired a well-aimed shot. The captain fell lifeless to the deck.

Rooster growled, "Put this chest in my quarters for now. We'll split all the treasure up even when we get back to camp." Charles watched and listened from the schooner's deck. He had heard of the pirate code of sharing all bounty equally. He also knew that this captain had no measure of honesty and was not planning on sharing this chest of treasure with his crew. It wasn't long before all the gold and silver plunder were on the pirate ship and it sailed away. They left the Spanish galleon empty of treasure and some of the sailors alive so they could later tell the story of the fearsome pirate raid. Rooster smiled proudly and fingered his red mustache. He fancied that he would soon become as famous as the pirate, Blackbeard.

"Redbeard," he proudly muttered. The name suited him.

A sly weasel, called Patch, walked over to the boy and peered at him with his one bloodshot eye. He noticed that the prisoner had finished cleaning the fish and yelled at him to go help drag the heavy chest to the captain's quarters. "You'll keep yer

Rooster & Groggins Scheme about the Treasure

slimy hands out of them chests, if ya know what's good for ya." He pointed his cutlass at Charles and grinned, showing his brown teeth. Charles nodded quickly, realizing that if he rubbed this one-eyed pirate the wrong way, he might be the next one to have one eye.

Later, while the pirates celebrated their new wealth with several kegs of rum, Rooster and Groggins ordered Charles to bring two private jugs of their fine ale to the captain's quarters. When he entered the cabin with the jugs, Rooster quickly slammed the chest lid shut, but not before the boy caught a glimpse of the silver and gold coins and glittering gems. The large wooden box was brimming over with treasure. Charles quickly lowered his eyes and pretended not to have seen anything.

Rooster turned to Charles and yelled angrily, "Didn't yer mama teach ya to knock?" Groggins threw an empty bottle at Charles, just missing his head but causing him to trip over a chair.

"Sorry, sir," Charles said hastily.

"You stupid, clumsy boy," Groggins barked. "Bring us them jugs 'afore you drop 'em or I'll wring yer scrawny neck!"

Charles quietly obeyed, thinking it might work to his advantage if the pirates thought him stupid.

Groggins winked his one beady eye at Rooster. In a rare mood of humor, he decided to play a trick on the boy. "Lift the chest, squirt, and carry it out of the way so's you don't trip over it. That is, if'n yer strong enough." Charles tried with all his strength to pick the chest up but could not lift the heavy box. Both men roared loudly and made fun of him.

"Boy, now git yerself to the galley and help Cook fix supper. When yer through, bring us some o' them bowls of that fish 'n tortuga soup he's making today. Mind you that the bread with it ain't moldy! And try not to trip over yor big feet and spill it!"

Charles retreated from the room just as Rooster was locking the chest. "No prying hands can get at this treasure now," the worthless villain boasted, swinging the key on his finger. Charles shut the door and hurried to the galley to help the cook.

As soon the meal was ready, Charles returned to the captain's quarters with a tray of two steaming bowls of fish and turtle soup and bread. He knocked on the door. Groggins opened it, grabbed the tray and pulled him inside with it.

Charles Brings Tortuga Soup to Rooster and Groggins

"Now, you stupid boy, move the table 'n chairs to the middle of the room so's we can have ourselves a proper dinner," Rooster bawled.

Groggins hissed, "Be quick about it, ya slimy perch, or we'll throw ya overboard!"

Charles kept his head lowered and obeyed quickly. Before he pulled the heavy table to the middle of the cabin, he picked up a piece of smudged paper, a quill pen and a bottle of India ink that had been left on it. The misspelled words, "Burd On Ilan" were clumsily printed on the paper. He knew as soon as he read it that they were making a map.

"Bring me that paper!" Rooster thundered. Then he jerked Charles up to him. "Can you read, fish bait?" He cast a furious look at his captive. Charles was overwhelmed by his decayed teeth and terrible breath but dared not back away.

Charles pretended not to be able to read. "Uh, no S-Sir, uh, I-I-I ain't never learned my, uh, l-letters." he replied. Groggins and Rooster laughed arrogantly at his admission and tossed the paper aside in full view. No need to hide it from this illiterate nitwit who couldn't even talk much less read.

"See," said Groggins, "I told ya he was brain damaged, Cap'n!" They both whooped.

School was expensive in the early 1800s and few children had the privilege of attending. Though it hadn't seemed important at the time, Charles was now thankful that his mother had taught him and his brothers and sisters to read from the Bible. Now, he was sure the captain and first mate were going to bury part of the treasure for themselves.

"Now slide the chest against the wall and git out of here, you blundering imbecile!" Groggins snarled.

Charles grabbed the chest's handles to slide it against the wall. Instantly, he could tell that the chest was only half as heavy as before, but he was quick-witted enough to keep his eyes down and show no surprise. He realized that the two scoundrels had already taken some of the treasure out and hidden it away. He wondered what the other pirates would do if they found out that half the treasure was gone.

Then spying a smaller wooden chest under Rooster's bed, he decided to keep as close a watch on Rooster and Groggins as he could. Perhaps they had transferred the missing gold to the smaller chest. Rooster was sly enough to know that their crew would not suspect that any had been removed from the original chest since it was still half full. They would have no way of knowing that it had been completely full of treasure.

Chapter 8:

Rooster & Groggins Bury the Treasure

The notorious pirates sailed the schooner south around the tip of Florida and then turned west into the Gulf of Mexico. Charles' ball and chain were left off now since there was nowhere that he could escape to except the open sea and the jaws of a waiting shark. He was amazed at the sight of the beautiful water. It was like none he had ever seen before--bright, clear aqua shimmering under the warm sun. Farther out, the sea turned to a deep blue and finally to a rich purple. It was said that the beaches here were pure white sand and looked much like salt.

The day before they reached Barataria Island off the Louisiana coast, the schooner dropped anchor and the crew was allowed to jump into the clear water for a swim and a much-needed bath.

"Keep a sharp eye out fer sharks! They be aplenty in these 'ere warm waters," Groggins yelled to the sailors.

They Allowed Charles to get in the water, too, since they were still far from shore. He was suspicious because Rooster never did anything nice for anyone. The men were happy and didn't seem so mean while they were in the water. They splashed and played like children but Charles did not trust them. He decided to stay to himself by the ship and under the schooner's jack ladder. The less the pirates noticed him, the less they thought of harassing him. The row boats were stored on deck right above the jack ladder in case the crew should ever have to make a hasty retreat from a sinking ship.

From his hiding place beneath the ladder, he could hear voices and realized Rooster and Groggins were standing above him on deck. They were talking, unaware that anyone was within earshot.

"Hurry up, mate. Let's git this chest stowed in the rowboat 'afore the crew gits back on board," Rooster instructed.

The heavier Groggins replied, panting, "Slow down, Cap'n, this gold's heavy. I'm doin' the best I can."

Charles quietly squeezed tighter between the hemp rope jack ladder and the side of the ship and sank low into the water, hoping no one would not see him. He was sure they were up to no good but knew he would pay with his life if they caught him listening. It was quiet for a moment except for the grunting of the hefty Groggins.

"Pull the canvas back and help me hoist the chest into the boat." Rooster ordered.

Charles held his breath because they were now directly above him. He heard the thud of something heavy being dumped into a rowboat. Then Groggins asked, "What if someone finds it 'afore tomorrow?" They covered the boat again.

The crafty captain always had an answer. "That be no problem. We'll accuse the mute kid of stealing some of the treasure. Then the men will deal with 'em!" They both chuckled.

Charles' heart was beating so loudly he was sure they would hear it, but neither looked over the side. He waited a few more minutes to be sure they were gone, then slid out from under the ladder and swam over to where the crew was, feeling safer with them now than by the ship. Suddenly, Stubby spotted two fins moving slowly toward them.

"Sharks!" He cried, and everyone swam, yelling and screaming, to the ship. They fought over who would be first up the jack ladder, knowing that one bite would take a leg off in an instant.

That night, before the boy went to sleep, he considered what he should do. He thought of his father and mother and what they would tell him. Then he felt the little gold cross around his neck and the ring and prayed for wisdom. It came to him that he could tell the crew about their captain and first mate's theft but, no doubt, Rooster would convince them that he had stolen the gold. He decided that he must keep his mouth shut until the pirates took him to the "Bos." Perhaps he could use this knowledge to buy his freedom.

The schooner continued west and dropped anchor at Barataria, an island in the swamps beside New Orleans. The "Bos" had many men and schooners under his command and used this island as his headquarters, according to what Charles had overheard the pirates say. Charles was swabbing the deck when he saw the cunning Groggins pull a small shovel from under his shirt and slip it quickly into the rowboat, thinking no one was looking. There were only five ships anchored near the island and no signs of life, but none of the pirates seemed to notice. The crew was excited and busily getting ready to go ashore to the nearby noisy New Orleans pubs and gambling houses. Charles realized that their Bos wasn't there because he had heard them brag about "Bos' thousand-man navy.

"You men chain the rascal so's he don't escape and we'll go check out the headquarters and find out if Bos is out on a raid!" Rooster yelled back to his men. Then Rooster and Groggins got into the rowboat and called for it to be lowered. They rowed toward the shore of Barataria. Rooster and Groggins were using this opportunity to bury their stolen treasure on the island without prying eyes and getting clean away with it.

Charles continued to scrub the deck but kept an eye on Rooster's curious actions. Rooster and Groggins headed to the house that served as the headquarters and talked to an old man who then accompanied them into the woods. No one else seemed to wonder about these strange events.

Charles was now sure that Rooster and Groggins were going to bury their smaller, wooden chest of treasure on this island! He wished he could see where they were digging but they had disappeared into the trees. He mentally marked the place where they disappeared. The crew thought that the captain was taking a box filled with bottles of rum to the Bos and so paid no attention to this theft of Spanish treasure going on right under their noses! And the "stupid boy" was not about to say anything.

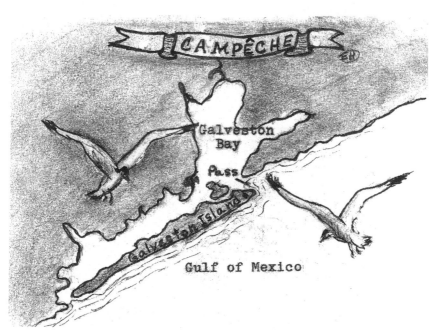

Campeche (Galveston Island) Camp

Rooster and Groggins rowed back a little later with the news that Bos and their band of buccaneers had been ordered away from Barataria by the United States Government. They had moved the headquarters to a place called Galveston Island, just off the coast of Texas, then a territory of Mexico. Groggins reported that the anchored ships had been left behind because they weren't seaworthy and needed repair, according to the old crippled pirate who lived on the wooded island. Charles wondered if they had killed the old man before or after they buried the treasure.

* * * * *

The year was 1814 and the United States President, James Madison, had finally decided that the huge pirate band must leave the New Orleans area and the United States once and for all. "Bos" and his men were already national heroes for helping the U.S. General, Andrew Jackson, save New Orleans from a British attack and for driving away the feared Spanish galleons. They had even received pardons for their patriotism but the government still considered them a threat. Rumors of pirate attacks on American ships had surfaced, however, and President Madison realized that the band of buccaneers had gotten out of hand. Faced with having to leave or be arrested, the pirate boss chose to move their headquarters to Galveston Island, Texas, which was then a part of Mexico.

* * * * *

Rooster and Groggins, both in extraordinarily good moods, announced to their men that they were going to follow Bos to the new headquarters. They gave them the choice of getting off the schooner at nearby New Orleans or going on to

Galveston with them. Rooster had thrown in his lot with the pirates four years ago and liked the easy money.

Many of the sailors wanted to get away from this cruel captain. "If'n we gits off here, can we collect our fair share of loot now?" asked Stubby, the bravest sailor. " I gots family here I'd like to see."

Rooster's good humor faded and his ugly face filled with rage. "You scallywags what wants to jump ship here gits nothing! The treasure will be split at Galveston fair and square." Charles wanted to laugh at Rooster's sudden righteousness. He knew that any gold left behind would go straight into Rooster's pockets.

"But, Cap'n," Stubby continued, "We helped raid the galleon. What's the difference if'n we gits off here or at Galveston? Some of the other men shyly agreed."

"You wants off? OK!" Rooster could see the threat of mutiny within his crew and screamed, "Throw the troublemaker overboard!"

He ordered three unwilling sailors to toss the big two-fingered man into the water and then, laughing, shot at him as he swam to the island. The rest of the men chose to stay on the ship so they could get their share of the Spanish loot when they reached the island.

* * * * *

Bos had chosen a good place for his new headquarters because Mexico owned Texas, including Galveston Island. The country had agreed that he could bring his band of men there and make camp in return for helping sink the hated Spanish Galleons. Galveston was a twenty-seven mile long, three-mile wide island, partially covered with salt cedar bushes, palms and scrub oak trees. It had a smooth, sandy beach on the south side facing the Gulf. The rocky, north side of the island bordered a deep, calm bay that faced the wilderness mainland of Texas. There was a narrow pass, between the east end of the island and the mainland that was just deep enough for their schooners to sail through, even at low tide. It was a perfect hiding place for buccaneers to drop anchor and dock their ships, however, it was hard for larger ships to maneuver through the pass at low tide.

The pirate leader gave Galveston the new name of *Campeche,* meaning "bayside," and he continued raiding Spanish Galleons in the Gulf and Caribbean from this new headquarters.

* * * * *

Rooster sailed his schooner out of the bay and into the Gulf of Mexico and headed west toward Texas. The evil captain and his awful first mate did not realize it, but they had made a fatal decision that day. All the while, Charles remained on board and under Hong Kong's guard.

When they reached Campeche, they dropped anchor in the harbor. The rowboats were lowered and the crew went ashore with the treasure chests because, according to the pirates' code, all treasure was split between everyone in their band. Rooster took young Tilton with him, pulling him along. Then he halted for a moment on the dark beach.

"All right, seascab, I'm gonna tell me own tale to Bos about how you came to be here and you ain't gonna say one word! You so much as breathe wrong an' I'll drag ya down to the water tonight and run you through with this 'er cutlass. Then I'll tie ya up and throw ya out there fer the crabs to eat piece by piece!"

Charles' legs nearly buckled beneath him when he heard the bloodcurdling threat. He knew that the wicked Rooster was not above such a gory end for him. He had always heard that pirates were evil to the core. The others might well just watch and celebrate while he died. He would continue his mute act. Bos was probably going to kill him anyway but perhaps with a quicker, kinder death.

Rooster drags Charles toward Pirate

"You listen to me, Stupid, and stay quiet!" whispered the wicked pirate, staring intensely into Charles' eyes, his breath hot on the boy's face. Then, just for good measure, Rooster drew his cutlass, still stained with blood from the Spanish Galleon attack, and jabbed it into the boy's back to give him a sharp taste of pain.

Charles knew better than to cry out, but he was so frightened he could not have uttered a single sound, even if he had wanted to. He nodded hard, having no reason to disbelieve this evil man. Rooster had already threatened his men and Charles had no doubt that Bos would believe his tale. Dragging the wounded boy along, the vain pirate strutted into the firelight with his first mate proudly marching behind.

A big campfire was burning and the well-dressed leader and many men were sitting around it laughing and talking and admiring the latest treasure that had been taken off a loaded Spanish Galleon. They shouted greetings when Rooster and Groggins walked into the flickering light. Then all mouths dropped open and all eyes watched as the haughty captain and his pompous first mate paraded their terrified young prisoner forward.

Chapter 9:

Meeting Bos Face to Face

*I*n spite of his fear, Charles could not help but be struck by the appearance of this revered leader, who was known as *Bos*. He was smartly dressed in a clean, black uniform, shiny black boots and a white ruffled shirt. He wore a large brimmed, black gentleman's hat with a long, fluffy, white ostrich feather attached. The man was striking with olive skin and a handsome Roman nose. He stood well over six feet tall, had coal black eyes and hair and heavy eyebrows. His black mustache and small, pointed beard were carefully groomed causing him to look, for the entire world, like a French aristocrat. The astonished boy suddenly realized that the man he was standing before was none other than the world famous privateer, Jean Lafitte!

* * * * *

Jean Lafitte was a Frenchman, born in the coastal city of Bayonne, France, in 1790, to a store owner and baker and to his wife. He was one of ten children of his French father, who was born in France, and his Spanish mother, who had come from the nearby country of Spain. He and his brothers attended a fine school run by priests and there they learned to read and write both languages, as well as English. But the boy loved the sea and, at the age of nine, ran away from home and hid on a ship. When he was discovered, however, he was kicked off the vessel.

Only Known Portrait of Jean Lafitte. Courtesy of Lafitte Museum, Huntsville, TX

"We don't take on children!" The captain barked at the boy. Jean's father soon found him there on the wharf and took him back home and back to school.

In 1802, when Jean was twelve, he left home again and hid aboard another ship bound for the islands of the Caribbean. This time he wasn't found until the ship was well out to sea, so he was allowed to stay on and work. After a long journey across the Atlantic Ocean, the ship docked in Santa Domingo, a seaport city of the Dominican Republic in the Caribbean Sea. Here Jean left the ship and lived for six years doing various jobs. Having had excellent schooling for the times, the brilliant lad spoke and wrote French, Spanish and English fluently and was able to do higher math. Within a short time, he had all the work he wanted translating and helping with shipping records.

When he was eighteen, he fell in love with a beautiful dark-eyed Spanish girl named Lucia. They were happily married and lived for several more years in Santa Domingo. Jean still loved the sea and finally saved enough money to purchase his own schooner. He and his wife were out sailing on it one day when Spanish Galleons attacked them. His beloved Lucia was killed in the gunfire, the ship sank and Lafitte escaped with only his life. His heart was broken and he vowed life-long revenge against Spain by becoming a buccaneer and attacking their ships at sea.

* * * * *

Jean Lafitte in Camp on Galveston Island

"Well, what have we here?" Lafitte inquired in his heavy French accent, cocking one dark eyebrow and glancing at his brother, Pierre. He had little fondness for either the conniving

Jay Rooster or Jim Groggins. But, feeling very important, the two scoundrels brought the boy before him.

Rooster stepped forward. His dirty, orange beard was clean and combed for once. He began to brag in detail about his cunning attack on the huge Spanish galleon, adding false accounts of his own bravery as he went. As he spoke and gestured dramatically to impress Lafitte, his men carried the Spanish chests of gold and silver, into the camp, sat them down and opened them in front of Bos' large, elegant chair. The eyes of every pirate widened as the treasure glittered in the firelight. Groggins indicated proudly that they had brought all the treasure back to be shared and Lafitte nodded and smiled. Then Rooster began to tell his story of how they had come by forty barrels of whale oil. Lafitte leaned forward in his chair, eager to catch every word of this recounting.

"Our main sail tore bad so's I had the men lower it onto the deck to sew it. Meanwhile, a galleon flying no flag comes right out of the blue and sees we was drifting. When they gits close, they starts shooting at us. Then I begins to think that the ship jes' might be a Spanish galleon in disguise. Me 'n Groggins 'n my brave men here finally got the sail up and managed to return fire on the rats. Turns out the galleon was on its way to Spain with a load of fine whale oil what they had stole off'n a innocent American whaler."

He was especially proud of pinning the whaler attack on a Spanish ship because the news of the whaler's disappearance would surely break soon. "When we overcame the galleon, we gits all the oil off'n the ship then we sinks the slimy riffraff down to Davy Jones' Locker. Now we're bringing all this fine oil for ya to sell." Rooster was thoroughly enjoying his performance and everyone's close attention.

He cleared his throat and began to speak again. "But the finest prize we brings ya is this ere' young boy who wus also a captive on the galleon. Judging by his clothes 'n jewelry, his family be rich and will pay high ransom for 'em!" Rooster and Groggins failed to notice Bos' growing suspicion. The other pirates sat as still as stones, hardly daring to breathe, for they, too, sensed that things were not adding up in Rooster's story. As he usually did, Lafitte asked Rooster's crew to stand up and vow that this account was true. This kept a captain from keeping back loot. A slight glance from Rooster and the crew quickly nodded and declared that this was exactly what had happened.

More relaxed now, Lafitte turned his attention to the lad. "Come forward, boy."

Charles stepped slowly forward, his eyes on the ground. He could feel Rooster's eyes glaring at him. He wished that this Frenchman would just tell him now if they were going to kill him or not. It was the not knowing that was so hard. He promised himself that he would continue to play dumb. Perhaps the act might save his life.

"Where did these men capture you?" Bos quizzed Charles.

No answer.

"Are you hungry?"

Still no answer. Rooster smiled, satisfied that his threats had worked well.

"He ain't too smart," Groggins interrupted. "We thinks sompin's wrong with 'is brain. He can't talk much at all." Charles continued to stand silently staring at his feet.

Every fiber in his body cried out to tell the mighty leader what had really happened, but Charles dared not trust this man either. If Bos knew the truth, he might decide that they needed to get rid of the evidence of Rooster's raid on the American whaler and kill him now.

Jean Lafitte signaled with a finger for one of his men to lean toward him and whispered something into his ear. Then he commended Rooster and Groggins for their bravery and honor in sharing all of the loot and invited them to sit down and eat. The conversation and laughing began again and many men came forward to congratulate the captain and his first mate.

The cook brought Charles a steaming bowl of shrimp and fish gumbo. The boy sat down on the ground and tried to eat the good soup, but the ground beneath him began to spin slowly, then faster and faster. Then his head began to whirl. The bowl slipped from his hands and he fell over onto the sand.

Charles Passes out on the Beach

*****

A blanket was brought and wrapped around Charles. "This boy seems to be in shock and he's wounded." Pierre exclaimed loudly as he noticed the blood on Charles' shirt. "Get him a bandage and some hot coffee!"

A little while later, Lafitte's messenger returned and whispered something in his ear. Unbeknown to Rooster and Groggins, the messenger and several men had rowed out to his schooner and checked the sail for damage.

Lafitte's dark eyes flashed with fire. He stood up, trying to control his mounting rage. The camp became silent when he yelled for Rooster and Groggins to come back and stand before him. No one moved as he unleashed a tirade of anger against the two pirates. "Your main sail is as good as new and has not been repaired. You have lied to me and these men tonight, you worthless weasels."

Both of the wicked pirates began to tremble and blubber denials. Several of Rooster's crew were brought forward. "This is your only chance. Tell me the truth now before I have all of you hanged!" The sailors, who were more afraid of Lafitte than of their captain, all began to speak at once. Soon the evil actions of the captain and his first mate came out.

"What flag was the whaler flying?" Looking at Charles, he yelled, "Did you take this boy off the American whaler? What did you do with the rest of the crew?"

Answers flowed fast and furious as the sailors told about Rooster's ordered attack. Then Bos stood in front of the evil pair. "How could you be so stupid? Your heads must be as empty as gutted fish! You know that I have given specific orders not to attack American ships! Your actions will cost us dearly when it becomes known!"

The two stood before their leader, totally shocked by his bristling contempt. Enraged, Lafitte ordered that Rooster and Groggins be put into chains and "taken care of" the next morning for disobeying his orders. Their knees buckled and they groveled in the sand.

"Get up! Act like men, if that is possible!" the French leader commanded.

*****

At that moment, Charles groaned and stirred. Tall Dan, Lafitte's trusted, old, friend, was sitting beside him putting a clean bandage on his back. Then he lifted the boy's head and held a hot cup of coffee under his nose. Charles opened his eyes, glad the world had quit spinning.

"Here lad, take some of this 'ere strong coffee and it'll bring ya back to yer senses."

Charles sat up and realized that it was still night. He must have passed out for only a few minutes. "Thank you," he muttered softly, still afraid to speak.

"Don't be afraid, lad. Old Tall Dan is right beside you. Ain't nothing nor nobody gonna hurt ya." He saw the boy looking around. "Take a gander over yonder." Dan pointed his bony finger. "Them's the two scoundrels what kidnapped ya. Look at 'em!"

On the other side of the campfire sat Rooster and Groggins, chained together and sobbing. Charles breathed easy for the first time in months. "What happened?"

"Bos is smarter than them rascals, by far. They thought they'd pulled the wool over his eyes but the tables is turned and the truth is out. Now they're gonna pay fer attacking your whaling ship. I'm sorry 'bout yer friends."

Old Tall Dan, one of Lafitte's Men & Charles' New Friend

"Thank you kindly, Tall Dan, Sir. I'm much obliged," Charles answered as he stood up and shook hands with the old pirate.

"Yer safe here and you're gonna be all right," Dan assured him. "Don't ya worry none. Now, I don't reckon I can say the same fer them two thieving scallywags." Seeing the boy's confusion, Dan continued, "See, Bos is a good and just leader. He is a privateer who works fer the U.S. Government. He has letters of permission from President Madison and Mexico to rid the seas of the thieving Spanish Galleons. The Spanish frigates steals Mexico's gold and attacks American ships, capturing workers to take back to Spain as slaves. We're allowed to keep all the booty we gets off the galleons an', in return, Bos promised that we won't attack no American ships."

Indeed, Tall Dan was right about the contract. President Madison was worried, though, about the size of Lafitte's band of men.

Chapter 10:

The Hempin' Jig

With a gesture of his hand, Lafitte summoned four men who appeared out of the darkness to take the two evil pirates away. Then suddenly, he changed his mind and called the boy to his side. He handed his flintlock pistol to Charles. "Boy, it is fitting and just, if you can stand, that you take these scoundrels to the jail. Some of my men will accompany you."

Rooster and Groggins stopped wailing and stared in horror when Charles, suddenly filled with strength, stepped before them. His hands shook as he lifted the heavy pistol. Then he remembered his friends who had so cruelly been put out to sea in rowboats and his courage returned. Standing tall for his fifteen years, he glared at the two evil men.

"Sirs," he declared loudly and seriously, "I have never killed anyone and I have no intention of harming you, but I am about to shoot in the place where you are standing. I suggest that ye move with haste toward jail right now."

With that, he aimed squarely at Rooster's chest and cocked the pistol. Instantly, the two began scurrying off to the jail, wailing loudly as they went. Lafitte and Pierre began chucking and then broke into loud laughter and slapped their knees.

The entire camp of pirates roared with laughter and shouting, "Well said, boy!"

When Charles returned to the camp, Lafitte called him over and asked, "What is your name, lad?" He looked intently at the boy in the firelight.

"Charles Tilton, sir," Charles managed to answer in a shaking voice. He could hear some of the pirates snickering at his obvious fear.

Lafitte glanced sternly in their direction and the laughter stopped. "And where is your home? How old are you, boy?" Lafitte's face softened as he questioned the boy.

Charles swallowed then spoke in a stronger voice, "New Hampton, New Hampshire, sir. I was on the whaler, *Evening Star*, when we were attacked. I was captured alone and, if this be August, I have turned fifteen."

Bos nodded. "I am sorry for what those men did. I cannot always control my men's actions, but I punish them severely when they disobey me." Lafitte looked into the boy's eyes. "It is said in France that green eyes are sign of strength. You are not only a brave boy but a very bright one to have out-smarted Rooster and Groggins by acting daft." He chuckled then patted Charles' shoulder and Charles knew that his words were sincere.

"Yes, sir," Charles said, still thinking of all his good friends, the whalers. "Thank you, sir."

Lafitte gazed into the campfire and rubbed his chin in thought. He knew that if they returned the boy to his home now, it would be an admission of piracy on an American vessel and the government would turn on them. The sharp-witted Frenchman quickly decided on a solution. He would take the lad on as a cabin boy, the safest job on a ship, for a while. He saw the boy was young and frightened and he firmly ordered the entire camp that no harshness or harm come to the lad under penalty of death then he offered Charles a job.

Lafitte gave a hand signal to the cook and ordered another big bowl of fish and shrimp gumbo for him. Immediately, the cook went to the big cook house and soon returned with a tray of steaming soup and bread. Charles hadn't realized how hungry he was until he began to eat the delicious food.

"So the gumbo meets with your approval?" Bos looked at the boy kindly.

"Yes, sir, it sure is better than weevil biscuits!" Charles grinned and replied between huge gulps. Again Jean Lafitte and his brother, Pierre, had a hardy laugh from this likable boy. After Charles had eaten his fill, they ordered a tent to be set up for him.

One of the pirates sitting by the campfire leaned towards Charles and said, "Aye, ya can cast yer eyes on them two pieces of trash come sunup. Them mangy seadogs'll be doing the *Hempen' Jig.*" Charles wondered but didn't ask what he meant.

Later that night, Hong Kong, the pirate who had worked on Rooster's ship, came to Charles' tent and brought him a worn, leather pouch from the jail. It contained all the possessions that Rooster and Groggins had carried on them. "Bos tell me to give you this 'ere pouch." The Chinaman continued, "This 'ere pouch may have some of yer belongings. He say even if it don't, ya keep it anyway. And he send you this silver piece of eight for your birthday."

Shifting his weight from one foot to the other, Hong Kong paused then cleared his throat. "I want say I sorry for harsh treatment I gave ya. I was jes doing what Cap'n Rooster tell me." He stared at the ground and his hands twitched nervously. He knew that a word from Charles to Bos could mean the end of his life.

"All right, but don't try it again," Charles said, trying hard to sound stern, as the jittery little man handed the pouch to him. Charles smiled to himself, knowing that all of Rooster's men would tread lightly around him from now on. Charles drew his slim body up as tall as possible and added, "Thank Bos for the coin and his kindness."

Hong Kong nodded his head. "Yes, sir." Then he hurried away, his long pigtail swinging behind. Somehow, the nervous pirate looked smaller to the boy.

Charles admired the silver coin but wondered what in the world was in the pouch. He pulled the two strings that held it closed together and opened it. Inside was a handful of coins and a dirty, folded wrinkled paper. As soon as he unfolded it, he knew that it was Rooster's map. Charles recognized the island of Barataria, identified with the letters

"Ilan" and a rough drawing. In the middle there was an X marked between three trees and a big rock. Charles' eyes widened and his heart pounded.

Only three people knew what this map stood for and two of them are now dead. Only I am left alive with the secret, he thought and decided to keep the secret for a while longer.

Sure enough, noise woke him up early the next morning. Charles came out of his tent. He saw a dark-haired figure and a figure with a bright orange beard climbing the gallows. When the board they stood on was pulled away, he turned away then looked again. He could not help but notice that their legs were kicking as they hung by the hemp ropes. His eyes wide, he realized that the *Hempen' Jig* was a disobedient pirate's Dance of Death.

Hempin' Jig

Chapter 11:

The Swashbuckling Pirate Life & A New Friend

Jean Lafitte was a very enterprising privateer, having gotten letters of marquee from both the United States President and Mexico to clear America and Mexico's coasts of the hated Spanish galleons. For this service, he was allowed to keep all the treasure from the galleons. The Frenchman wasn't interested in killing the sailors of these ships and, in fact, most of them chose to join his buccaneering band.

Strange as it may seem for a buccaneer, Jean Lafitte was known for his courtesy and good manners toward ladies and his kindness to children. He was well liked by people who met him and had even once entertained Jane Long, the well-known Mother of Texas, aboard his ship. She later described the wonderful French banquet, his flawless manners, and delightful conversation. The people of New Orleans also liked him and entertained him often at their parties and banquets while he had his headquarters at Barataria Island. He was even considered a national hero because he and his men helped Andrew Jackson win the Battle of New Orleans against the British invasion there in 1812.

Jean Lafitte liked Charles, took him under his wing and made him a cabin boy. Charles, thankful not to be sold as a slave or held for ransom, eagerly performed the tasks of keeping Lafitte's cabin tidy, washing his clothes, and serving his meals. In return Lafitte, hoping to buy time before the United States learned of Rooster's attack on the *Evening Star*, paid him a beginning sailor's wage that he could save up until he had enough money for passage home. The boy reminded Jean of himself long ago in France.

Charles loved the sea and was treated kindly by all the pirates aboard the vessel, so going home became an event in the distant future when he had the money. Every day, when he had finished his chores, he could roam about the ship, listen to the crew's stories, and learn about the schooner. Some days, they would lower the anchor and swim in the warm Gulf water. Charles learned to dive and sometimes even won the contests.

Charles liked this exciting, carefree life on the ship with the smell of salt spray in his nostrils and the feel of the cool sea breeze blowing on his face. Pirates were free to roam where they pleased, do what they wanted and enjoy life. He had been raised by good parents and knew that this was not exactly the lifestyle they would have chosen for him, but he was in a faraway place with no funds to return home so he decided to make the best of his situation. And besides he liked Bos!

Lafitte's band of pirates continued to cruise about the Gulf of Mexico and the Caribbean, preying on foreign ships, as the privateer marquees or letters from the United States and Mexico gave them permission to do. Lafitte favored the huge, slow moving Spanish galleons, loaded with stolen Mexican gold and silver and heading back to Spain.

The buccaneers watched from afar for a slow ship that had been separated from the others by night or bad weather. They would raid these galleons and often the Spanish sailors would vote to join Lafitte.

The group declaring allegiance to Lafitte grew larger after the privateer moved his base to the uninhabited Galveston Island. The pirate group soon numbered well over a thousand men and almost a hundred vessels. Booty was divided among the men according to the rank of their jobs and according to any of their injuries. They were paid in pieces of eight, which were silver

Injury Compensation

In pieces of eight

1 piece of eight = $0.96 USD

Loss of an eye: 100

Loss of right arm: 600

Loss of left arm: 500

Loss of a finger: 100

Loss of right leg: 500   Loss of left leg: 400

Injury Compensation Chart

Spanish coins, and in gold coins, called doubloons, in gold bars and in gems, which had been taken from the Spanish Galleons. Lafitte was a good leader and earned the respect of his men for his fairness and generosity.

In return for Charles agreeing to work for him for two years, Lafitte raised his salary. Charles was thrilled with the wages, for the money was more than he had ever dreamed of, and he stored the coins away in socks behind a loose board in back of his hammock. The money was safe because every man feared the wrath of their leader, knowing they would pay with lashes on their back if they stole from their own shipmates. Pirates had a high code of honor among their own.

Campeche became a small city filled with stores selling goods and guns from the Spanish galleons, slave traders, casinos, saloons, restaurants and warehouses. Many merchants from New Orleans and other towns came to Campeche to buy goods for low prices. James Bowie, the famous hero who died at the Alamo, was just one of the buyers who came often to the island with his brother to make purchases. They then would sail back to New Orleans to sell them.

Jean Lafitte had a large, plantation style, red brick home built near the harbor entrance and named "Moulin Rouge," which was French for "Red House." He shared it with his brother, Pierre, Pierre's wife, her sister and their children. Here Lafitte set himself up as Governor of the island and head of the huge band of buccaneers.

Charles liked his new friends. There was old One-eyed Jack who taught him to play the harmonica, and Jumbo, the cook, who was very jolly. Then there was Stumpy, who had a wooden peg where his left leg used to be. Stumpy taught Charles to read a compass and to steer by the stars. Old Cricks liked to whittle and enjoyed making little wooden animals for Charles.

Of all the pirates, it was Tall Dan who was Charles' favorite. He could dance a jig and do back flips, but what fascinated the boy were his endless tales of adventures, mysteries from faraway lands and stories about Indians. They became fast friends in a very short time.

One day, the sailor on watch in the crow's nest, spotted some men on a deserted beach waving at their ship. "Ahoy, men off the starboard bow!"

They sailed closer and realized that the group included several men and a boy. Charles Louis Cornea, a thirteen year-old French boy, was one of the survivors of a storm that had sunk their French merchant ship on its way to New Orleans. They had floated on rubble and managed to reach a deserted beach. The pitiful group was hauled onto the schooner only half alive, but with some water and food, they soon came around.

Jean Lafitte gave a huge sigh and exclaimed, "We will soon be running a boys' home if this keeps up!" Then he laughed loudly, slapping his hat on his knee, and both boys knew that he was only joking.

Lafitte quickly dubbed Charles Louis Cornea by his second name, Louis, since they already had one Charles. Over time, the men also changed Charles' name to the more informal *Charlie*. After the work was done, the boys spent a lot of time playing rock chess, whittling, and fishing. Louis spoke only a little English but soon Charles taught him the language and Louis taught Charles some French. They became good friends and determined to work hard and enjoy their lot in life right now. The French lad and the American boy formed a bond of friendship that would remain for the rest of their lives.

Whenever Lafitte walked by, he would always greet Louis in French and ask how he was doing. "Bonjour, Louis. Comment-allez vous?"

"Tres bien, merci, M'sieur Bos." Louis would answer that he was fine and thanked *Mr. Bos,* as he called him. Lafitte smiled to hear his native tongue.

One day the boys stood at the rail looking out toward the horizon. Charles remarked,   "One day, I shall go back to my family in New Hampshire and you will also go home."

After a pause, Louis softly commented, "No, Charlie, I will never go back to France."

Astonished, Charlie looked at his friend. "Why, Louis?" He gasped in disbelief.

"Because I have no family. My mother died the year before I left to sail with my father and he died in the storm that wrecked our ship," Louis said, matter-of-factly. "I have decided that I will stay in America and make my life here."

"Then you shall be my brother and come home with me!" Charlie said, resolutely. "My parents will be glad to have my best friend as another son." He patted Louis' back and Louis smiled in gratitude.

Louis looked squarely at his friend and nodded. "Merci, mon ami, merci. Thank you, my friend, thank you." Charles now noticed a sparkle in his friend's eyes that he had not seen before. He thought that maybe it was hope and a reason for living.

Chapter 12:

Charles Reveals His Secret

Charlie and Louis liked the swashbuckling, pirate life and stayed with Jean Lafitte for many exciting adventures. They liked their leader and the free lifestyle that buccaneering allowed. Pirates could do what they wanted whenever they wanted! It was every boy's dream. They learned to fight with cutlasses, short swords they carried in scabbards on their belts. Tall Dan taught them to shoot muskets and soon each boy was issued one for his own. Charles taught Jumbo to cook hasty puddin' like his mother made and One-Eyed Jack taught both of them how to make the schooner sail in different directions and how to tie sailor's knots.

One day, Charles decided to share his long-kept secret about Rooster and Groggin's buried treasure with Louis. He reasoned that he couldn't sail alone all the way to New Orleans, even in the smallest sloop. He would need someone he could trust to help so he revealed his secret to his good friend. Louis' eyes widened as he listened to the story.

"They took about half the treasure out of that chest for themselves," whispered Charles. "They slipped it off the schooner and put it in the rowboat. When they came back to the ship later, the box and the shovel were gone. I know the gold and silver are hidden on Barataria Island near New Orleans and I want you to go with me to find it. If you will, I will split it evenly with you."

"Sacre Miracle! You are sure that the box had treasure in it?" Louis exclaimed.

"On my honor! I'm sure that I saw the treasure when they had the lid of the chest open and later I felt the lighter weight of the chest when I moved it for Groggins. I also heard them hoisting the box into the rowboat. They smuggled it off the boat right under the other pirates' eyes, smooth as silk!" Charles replied. "It is a small treasure, but will surely be enough for both of us."

Charles pulled Rooster's dirty folded map out of the pouch he carried around his neck and showed it to Louis. The boys swore each other to silence and agreed that, whenever they saved enough money to get a schooner, they would sail back to the island and find the treasure.

Lafitte treated Charles and the younger Louis more like sons than employees. He always had a ready smile and kind word for them. He found both of them to be hard working, loyal, smart and honest, and he rewarded them with raises in pay and rank. They could both read and write, something that most of the men could not do, so they were a great help reading maps and figuring distances.

Whenever the pirates raided a Spanish galleon, Lafitte would order the two young boys to stay on board his ship, write down what was brought on and help carry the booty down into the hold. When the treasure was split Charles and Louis received one part, which was every pirate's fair share. Lafitte took three parts and the officers got two parts. If any man lost a limb, he received four parts and if he was killed in battle, his family received ten parts. This was the pirates' code of fairness.

* * * * *

Three exciting years flew by and one day, when he was eighteen, Charles was promoted to the rank of boatswain, an officer in charge of rigging, anchors, and sails and of calling the crew to duty every morning. He was respectfully and fondly addressed as *boss'n*, short for boatswain, by the other pirates.

Louis was thrilled to become a *powder monkey*, the title given to the men in charge of the job of cleaning and loading the cannons with gunpowder. Lafitte had noticed that Louis, now sixteen, was a good shot and had excellent aim with a cannon, so he had begun grooming him to be a Master Cannoneer, an officer.

Trade in pirated goods in Campeche had reached an all-time high. The bay was filled with ships and goods taken on the high seas. Even the warehouses on the island could not hold all the spoils so crates, furniture and bales were piled high on the beaches. Campeche attracted more pirates and adventurers all the time claiming allegiance to the famous buccaneer. Houses dotted the island since some of the buccaneers even brought their wives and families to live there.

Charles decided it was time to tell Jean Lafitte the secret that only he and Louis had known for three and one-half years. He revealed the story about Rooster and Groggins and the treasure chest. Then he showed his leader the map and asked permission to go to Barataria, find the treasure and bring it back to Campeche to split.

"Charlie, why are you telling me about this treasure when you could go find it and keep it all for yourself?" Lafitte fingered his black mustache thoughtfully.

"Sir, you have been kind and like a father to Louis and me. I know about the policy of splitting all booty evenly. I would be a slimy scoundrel, indeed, if I plotted to cheat the man who had saved our lives and has been so good to us."

Lafitte listened carefully and smiled. He was proud of this boy who seemed like a son. Finally, he replied, "Charlie, you have become an honorable man and I admire you for that. However, since the treasure's whereabouts has not been discovered by anyone but you and it has not been brought here to our headquarters, as I see it, there is no need for anyone else to share in it. No, if you find the treasure, it belongs to you and you alone."

"Thank you, sir!" Charles could hardly believe his ears.

"I have an idea. I will lend you one of my schooners for two weeks so you can go and search Barataria for your treasure. Choose eight men to help sail it but tell them only that you are going to New Orleans for some wares for Bos."

Charles was overwhelmed. "Sir, are you sure?"

"Of course! You have become a young man now and it is time for you to learn to command a ship. I will give you money for some fine New Orleans rum and cigars so you will have a bona fide reason to go. Sail under the American flag and dock the schooner at the New Orleans port. The island is only a stone's throw away. The sailors will all soon head to the town's taverns. When they have all left the ship, you and Louis take the rowboat over to the deserted island alone. There you can search for your treasure without fear of the others knowing about it."

"Yes, sir!" Charles responded. He was so excited that he could hardly stand still.

"Just one more thing. Talk little and watch much. Thieving eyes and hands are always all around!"

Charlie tried to thank his friend for his generosity and good advice, but Lafitte would accept no thanks for doing the fair and right thing. "You serve me well and work hard. I wish you success in your venture." Then he rose from his chair and shook hands with Charles. "Bon Voyage," he added, wishing the boy a good trip.

Charles' chest swelled with pride as he later thought of Lafitte's rare compliment. It was hard to believe that Lafitte would entrust him with a schooner. Yes, he was a good and kind friend. Charles told Louis about their good fortune and they began planning the trip immediately. He told Louis to recruit twelve men to help them sail to New Orleans.

Schooner

Chapter 13:

Search for the Buried Treasure

One sunny morning the next week, Charles, Louis and twelve sailors set sail on *Black Jack* at high tide. Lafitte had announced his orders for rum and cigars loudly to the men and told them that this would be Charles' first time to command a ship. The other pirates sent him off with shouts and well-wishes.

The sailing weather was good. The third day into the voyage, Charles happened to notice Hong Kong among the crew. He was not pleased but there was no turning back now. Charles warned Louis to watch him because he did not trust the scoundrel.

When the ship's lookout spotted the port of New Orleans, Charles ordered that the sails be trimmed. Soon they lowered the anchor into the water beside the city's dock. The sailors were anxious to leave the ship and have free time in the town so it wasn't long before they had all left the schooner.

Charles and Louis went into town and purchased the rum and cigars then took the items back to the ship and locked them in the hold. They checked to be sure no one was watching from the wharf then they took two shovels from the tool rack and put them into one of the rowboats. The boys lowered the boat into the water and climbed down the jack ladder.

"All right, Louis," Charles said grinning, "Let's go!" He took hold of the oars and rowed to the nearby Barataria Island. All the while, Louis kept an eye out to see if they were being watched, but no one seemed to have noticed them.

They waded ashore the deserted island and pulled the boat onto the beach between some rocks to hide it. As they walked up the beach toward the woods, Charles pulled the map out of his shirt. "It shows three trees and a large black rock just west of them. We need to search for those landmarks. You head out to the left and I'll go right. Let's meet back here in an hour."

"Good enough," Louis replied nodding. "Let's go."

They headed in opposite directions carrying small shovels and watching for the big rock and any signs of life. Sure enough, it wasn't long before Louis spotted a large black rock. A few yards away from it were three oak trees so he began to dig. Suddenly, the shovel hit something that made a clinking sound. Louis dropped to his knees and began digging with his hands.

"I've found the treasure!" Louis said aloud. Then he shouted, "Charlie, over here, Charlie!" Suddenly, he heard a voice from the dense trees in back him.

"So you finally find Rooster and Groggin's stash," sneered Hong Kong. Louis turned his head and saw the crewman named Hong Kong pointing a flintlock pistol at him. "I saw map before I give it to Charlie two years ago. I knew if I wait long enough he come back to get treasure so I sign on when you ask for volunteers. He not know I watching him all this time." Hong Kong laughed a loud evil laugh over his cleverness.

Louis and Hong Kong Fight to the Death

Charles had heard Louis' call and came running with the shovel in his hand, but he stopped short in the brush when he heard the familiar, cruel laugh. He quietly worked his way around behind Hong Kong who was bragging about having read the map. The scoundrel had been patiently waiting for this chance to get the treasure for himself.

The pirate was so busy boasting that he failed to hear Charles slipping up behind him. Suddenly Charles slammed the shovel down on Hong Kong's head and he dropped the pistol and fell dazed to the ground. Louis ran over to grab it, but at the same second, the Chinaman regained his senses and also reached for it. Both of their hands locked around the weapon and they began to wrestle in a fight to the death. Charles was able to give Hong Kong two more hard hits. Although the vicious pirate was screeching and bleeding, he would not let go. He shouted curses and oaths at Louis as they rolled over and over in the dirt.

Hong Kong finally managed to cock the pistol with the barrel pointed toward the Louis' chest. Charles tried to whack him again but they were tumbling so fast that he feared he would hit his friend and cause him to loosen his grip. At last, Charles landed another hard blow with the shovel. It hit on Hong Kong's shoulder with a mighty cracking sound. The pirate's grip suddenly loosened enough for Louis to twist the gun upward.

"Let go of the gun and I will not harm you!" Louis cried. The two men spun into a standing position, their hands still locked together around the weapon as they whirled around and around in the rising dust.

"Never! You die today! The treasure be mine!" Hong Kong hissed. His piercing, evil eyes were locked on Louis'. At that moment, there was a gunshot and they both fell to the ground and lay motionless, their arms still locked around the pistol.

"Louis, are you alive?" yelled Charles. He was not sure which one had been shot. He bent over his friend, his eyes wide with horror.

Slowly, Louis stirred and pulled himself up to his knees. Blood covered his shirt. "I'm all right, mon ami," he panted. "The blood is his but I did not mean to take his life."

"Louis, you had no choice. He attacked you and would have surely killed both of us. Besides you didn't do this alone. I beat him with the shovel."

"Well then, perhaps you, rather than I, killed him." Louis cocked his eyebrow and gave a tired smile.

From the bushes, the boys heard a shrill giggle and quickly grabbed the weapons, readying themselves to fight yet another pirate. But a crippled, old man hobbled through the thick palmettos and out into the clearing. "No need to trouble yerselves with guilt over this weasel's death because neither one of ya killed the sea scum. 'Twas old Joseph 'ere and me trusty long rifle what took the riffraff's worthless life."

Charles blurted out, "You're the crippled pirate that stayed on the island when Lafitte moved his headquarters to Galveston!"

"Aye, that be me. *Crazy Joe* they call me," he replied, grinning. He sensed Charles' politeness in not using his nickname. "And I still lives here alone. Others stays away 'cause they think old Joseph is daft." He giggled again. "Jean Lafitte, hisself, gave the headquarters house to me for me home," the white bearded man added proudly. He limped over to the astonished boys and shook their hands.

Turning Hong Kong over, he nodded his head. "I knows this sorry rascal, for a fact. Never could be trusted and mean to the core. Yer lucky I happened along from rabbit huntin' and reckoned you boys needed some help from ole Betsy and me." He held up his rifle and laughed again.

Charles looked at Louis then opened the map for Joseph to see. "Sir, we are the rightful owners of this treasure and want to repay you for saving our lives by splitting this gold and silver with you." Louis agreed with a hardy nod.

They lifted the chest out of the hole and Charles gave the lock several whacks with the shovel. The rusty lock broke and Louis pulled open the lid. The three of them stood and stared with their mouths open wide. There lay gold doubloons, beautiful pearls and emeralds and silver pieces of eight all glittering brightly in the sunshine.

"Look at that treasure! There must be a small fortune here!" Joseph exclaimed.

Louis yelped, "Ohhh! Pinch me, mon ami, my friend! Am I dreaming?"

"No dream! It's real all right and it belongs to the three of us," Charles exclaimed. They picked up handfuls of doubloons and let them fall through their fingers and back onto the pile of treasure.

"I can't believe it. The three of us are rich! Rich!" Louis gasped.

"And rightfully so, for Jean Lafitte gave us permission to keep it!" answered Charles. He remembered Bos' words. The boys and old Joseph laughed and slapped each other on the back over their good fortune.

Then Charles told Joseph the story of how he was captured by Rooster and Groggins and of seeing them take the treasure ashore. Louis finished the story of the two evil pirates presenting Charles for ransom to Lafitte, of Bos hanging them and then giving the pouch and map to Charles, and later of Bos lending them a schooner to come and search.

"Aye, I wager that Hong Kong saw it too and weaseled 'is way onto the schooner you sailed 'ere." Both boys nodded. "You've both been through a lot, but yer young and you can now make sumpin' good of yer lives. It's nice of you to offer but

I want only as much gold as I can put in my little huntin' sack, if'n you don't mind. 'That will stay me well right 'ere for the rest of my life."

When Charles and Louis began to insist that he take his third, the old man said, "If I takes too much, someone might get wind of it when I spends it in town and I'd have to shoot another rascal. Hch, heh, heh," the old man giggled again and slapped his knee.

With that, Crazy Joe limped over to the chest and filled the little canvas sack with doubloons. He turned back toward the boys. "I'm beholden to ya. You two are honest young men. I wish ya both the good lives ya deserve. Now take yer rightful treasure and scat! I'll bury Hong Kong so's no one will ever know about this unpleasant incident. Oh, and tell Bos *Good Sailing* fer me." Then he ambled away, hobbling and giggling, the coins jingling as he threw the sack over his shoulder. Charles looked at Louis and they both shook their heads in amazement.

The boys quickly carried the box to the rowboat and rowed back to the *Black Jack*. They climbed the jack ladder up to the deck and, after making sure none of the sailors had returned early, they hoisted the rowboat and box up onto the ship. Charles suggested that they store their treasure under the bed in the captain's quarters. He remembered that tactic had worked well for Groggins and Rooster. They hauled the booty into the cabin and slid it under the bed. Louis grabbed a folded quilt and laid it over it to completely hide it.

"There, that should be all right until we get back to Campeche. The sailors aren't allowed in the captain's cabin unless invited, so our treasure should be safe and sound here," whispered Charles and Louis agreed. Then they went out on deck to think about today's events and await the sailors' return. Each boy was also thinking of the things he would do with his newfound wealth.

* * * * *

Early the next morning, as the crew made ready to set sail, Charles stood at the rail looking toward Barataria Island. There on the shore, he suddenly spotted Crazy Joe waving. Charles returned the wave and smiled, thinking, "Crazy like a fox." He knew he and Louis would not be alive had it not been for the quick thinking and actions of the old man. The crew raised the sails and their lives went on as usual, no one seeming to care or even remember that the disagreeable pirate was missing, since pirates came and went at will. That day, however, Charles and Louis' lives were forever changed.

When the *Black Jack* sailed into the harbor at Campeche, Jean Lafitte came out on the beach to greet them. As they rowed up to the beach, he gave Louis and Charles a wide smile. "Did you bring the back our treasure?" He yelled loudly over the waves for everyone to hear. Both boys gulped and stuttered, wondering why he could give their secret away! Then Lafitte quickly added, "We are in serious need of that rum and those fine cigars. Those are our treasures for the day!" All of the pirates cheered at his joke.

Charles and Louis suddenly understood that their cunning leader was making a joke and, at the same time, asking if they had been successful. Both of them replied in unison, "Yes sir, we brought back the treasure!"

"Well, we must hide it well so thieving hands won't take it from us. I think Maison Rouge is the perfect place," Lafitte continued, chuckling. He winked and laughed again as he looked at the wood crates of cigars and rum. Then he looked directly into Charles eyes and nodded to make sure he understood the double meaning. Charles returned it.

During the night, after the campfire had died down to red coals and the other men were asleep, Charles and Louis slipped back onto the ship and retrieved the box. They rowed it to shore a good half-mile from the camp then carried it up to Lafitte's big home and buried it on the north side, right next to the chimney wall. "There, we hid it right where Bos told us to—at his house!" whispered Charles. They both grinned from ear to ear.

Lafitte Burns Campeche

Chapter 14:

Campeche Ablaze~~1820

"Bos! Bos!" A man came running into the camp one afternoon and pointing toward the Gulf. "American Navy ships on the eastern horizon!"

The United States Government no longer needed the buccaneers to protect America's coast and had decided to drive them off the island. They sent a fleet of armed ships to Lafitte's headquarters at Campeche in 1820. The large, heavy vessels could not squeeze through the shallow harbor until high tide. The pirates knew that they would be able to sail into Galveston Bay as soon as the water level rose in the morning. For now, the fleet of Naval ships sat two miles off the coast waiting.

That evening, Lafitte had eight huge treasure chests that had not yet been divided carried from his house to the beach. First, he gathered all his men around the big campfire, held their last meeting and divided the schooners among his officers. Then he had the heavy chests of Spanish gold doubloons, silver pieces of eight and gems opened and began dividing the booty among all the men. Lafitte was generous, also rewarding his men for their loyalty and for injuries with extra pay.

Charles, who was now twenty and a boatswain officer, was thrilled to receive Lafitte's smaller, older ship, the *Black Jack*. He had sailed on it many times and liked the sturdy schooner.

Even though it was older than some of the others, it was well built. Louis had not risen to the rank of officer yet, so did not receive a boat, but he was happy to receive a generous amount of gold and silver coins, like all the other men. The amount paid to each man was enough to help him start a fine new life.

Charles sat in the firelight and listened to the mighty leader, whose strong face was now lined with sadness. "Men," he began in a booming voice and perfect English. "America's President Madison, himself, gave us a marquee and permission to rid their coast of the Spanish galleons. We did this just as their government instructed us to do." The men cheered in agreement.

He continued, "But now that the threat is gone, the government has turned on us and has sent the Navy to force us away from these shores. You must now scatter to evade the American ships. Cross the bay and hide anywhere on the mainland or sail out into the Gulf to another country. If you are caught, you will be arrested and taken to stand trial in the United States. Take any of the wares to your liking from the storehouses but make sure you are gone before the sun comes up, for shortly after that, the tide will rise high enough for the Navy ships to enter the harbor." Then he shook hands with the men in his huge following and wished them a long and good life.

Charles chose two close friends, old Tall Dan and Jose, a young trustworthy sailor who had come from Mexico to join Lafitte's band two years ago, to sail on his boat with Louis and him. Since he was planning only to cross Galveston Bay and sail up the Trinity River, he knew he could do it with this small crew.

They put all of their belongings aboard the *Black Jack* and made the schooner ready to sail with the stars for direction.

Later that night, after the campfire had died out, the others were catching nine winks, Charles and Louis scurried quietly in the darkness down the beach then across it to Lafitte's house. There, they hastily dug up their box of treasure, carried it to an empty rowboat, and rowed it out to the schooner. Once on board, they hid the little chest, as they had before, under the bed in the captain quarters.

Everyone was up and stirring long before daylight. The men watched and wondered as Lafitte picked up a stick of burning wood from the campfire. He held it up high and walked to his own large Moulin Rouge home. He had lived happily here for six years with his brother, Pierre, Pierre's wife, her sister and their four children, all whom he had sent earlier to New Orleans. He stood silently for a moment, perhaps remembering the good times and then, to the men's shock, threw the torch high up onto the wood shingle roof. When the roof began to burn, he turned and ordered the men to set fire to every building and all the cargo left on the island. The pirates would leave nothing for the United States Navy to take. The fires of Campeche crackled and reached higher and higher into the dark sky.

Charles watched and remembered another terrible blaze years ago, when the *Evening Star* had burned. He felt a strange, sad loss this time, as well, for he knew that another exciting chapter of his life was coming to an end, and a new chapter was about to begin.

Chapter 15:

Goodbye, Jean Lafitte

In March of 1820, the huge band of buccaneers prepared to part ways in the early morning darkness. Charles and Louis took only a few of the goods from the warehouses since they had gold. They readied the schooner with the help of their two friends, then rowed back to the beach. Jean Lafitte was standing in the midst of his officers shaking hands in the pre-dawn light when Charles and Louis walked up to him. He first took each of them by the hand and then gave them warm hugs. "Mon amis! My two boys have now grown up to be men," he said, looking proudly at them. You now have the resources to make something good of your lives. What do you think you will do?"

Louis spoke up. "Charles and I both like the land around the Trinity River here in Texas but he wants to go home to New Hampshire to visit his family for a while. I have decided to search the area for some good ranch land near the Trinity and invest my gold in many fine cattle and a home."

Charles shared the rest of their plans and Louis nodded in agreement. "We plan to build great homes like the Maison Rouge. I want to build mine on the bank of the river, buy more schooners and start a hauling business for farmers and ranchers to Galveston."

Lafitte listened intently and smiled. He took pride in these boys who had been like the sons he had never had. He hated to see them part ways after six happy, adventurous years, but knew they must pursue their own lives as he had done so many years ago.

"Boys, those are good plans and I am sure you will succeed. I wish the very best for you both! I know the Trinity area well, so perhaps we shall see one another again some day. Goodbye. Au Revoir!" Charles and Louis sadly bid him farewell. Jean Lafitte had been like a father and good friend to both of them.

While the buildings of Campeche were still burning, the forty men who had been chosen to go with Lafitte hoisted the sails of *The Pride*, his large, new schooner. He stood on the deck, the white ostrich feather on his large black hat blowing gently in the wind, and waved to all of his men. A great "Hurray" went up among them as their fearless leader's ship glided out into the semi-darkness toward the Gulf of Mexico. That was the last the pirate band ever saw of their infamous friend and buccaneer, Jean Lafitte.

Schooner

The men boarded the schooners and sloops and began parting ways. They sailed the ships out into Galveston Bay before the first light of dawn ahead of the naval ships. They all realized that their exciting days of pirating with Lafitte had come to an end. It was also the end of an exciting era in American History.

When the sun rose over the island that morning, the United States Naval ships sailed on the high tide into the bay. They searched for the pirates' schooners but could not find them. The smaller, faster ships had sped away before the big, heavy Naval ships could enter the harbor. All that was left were smoldering remains of buildings and stacks of burned wares. Every single man and their leader, Jean Lafitte, had vanished from Galveston Island during that fateful night.

Some historians say that Lafitte went to the Mexican Yucatan or deep into the Caribbean and lived there until he died. Others declare that he slipped back into the United States through New Orleans, married, and lived quietly until the end of his days.

Annie, the spirited, pioneer girl whom Charles would marry, later remembered that twice over the years, a delightful, tall Frenchman with black hair and a mustache tied his boat at their Trinity River dock and came in for short visits. His gracious manners and conversation always fascinated her. Charles always introduced him as his old friend, "Jacque Noir." Although no one thought to ask, the name simply meant *Black Jack*. Perhaps he was just an old friend from Charles' pirate days or could it have been his good friend, Jean Lafitte?

Chapter 16:

*Escaping and Hiding the **Black Jack***

Charles and his three friends, Louis, Juan, and Old Tall Dan, sailed the old *Black Jack* out into Galveston Bay. Lafitte have been more than generous to give the schooner to Charles because not only was it a good, dependable ship but it had four cannons and a solid copper deck covering that kept the schooner safe from enemy cannon balls. Charles had come to respect and admire his privateer friend, Jean Lafitte, and determined to live a life that would make him proud.

They crossed the bay and, checking to be certain they hadn't been followed, turned the ship into the Trinity River. Charles and Louis had sailed up this river many times with Lafitte and knew about a hard-to-find lake. Charles turned the schooner into Old River and, in a short while, steered it into a small, secluded lake, which he christened *Lost Lake.* He then slowly guided the boat in among the tall cypress trees that grew in the water. They felt well hidden from the Navy but still needed to be careful not to give their position away.

Juan and Tall Dan began quietly rowing some of the supplies ashore while Charles and Louis went to the captain's quarters and took their sacks of treasure from the chest. They had divided the Barataria treasure that Lafitte had allowed them to keep and now each boy had three hundred doubloons and silver pieces of eight from the treasure. They also had their pay and money from the spoils which Bos had divided with them. The young men rolled the bags of treasure up inside of the rugs they had brought from the warehouses. Then they rowed the rugs, along with loads of supplies, to shore, making sure to keep their treasure separate, knowing there was no need to mention it.

Black Jack Mast in Lost Lake

The four men unloaded the schooner in just a few hours. They feared that the government ships would send smaller boats up the river and find this lake, so Charles made a sad decision. After hearing the naval cannons booming louder and closer and unloading what they needed from the ship, they they scuttled the old schooner by chopping holes in the ship's bottom and sinking it. They watched sadly as the trusty *Black Jack* slowly sank into the deep, dark water. It was now quite out of sight, except for the mast with its crow's nest sticking up out of the water among the big cypress trees that grew in the lake. The four men felt safe for the time being but shuttered every time they heard the navel cannons, knowing they were shooting at some of their friends.

Satisfied that the Navel ships could not find them, the men made camp that night on the shore of the lake but decided not to build a fire. The next day the sounds of the Navy cannons booming slowed and finally stopped. They knew that the government ships had given up searching for them, so they built a small campfire and cooked some of the food they had brought. Tall Dan cut an animal skin from the ship into four pieces. Then the men heated their knives in the fire and, with the hot knives, burned maps into the skins.

The four friends split up the valuable objects they had salvaged from the schooner and their booty from Lafitte and decided to bury all of it there on the lake's shore. Then they all vowed to meet back at the same place in one year to the day to dig up the valuables and perhaps to dive down to the ship for the cannons and some of the larger items. There was no way they could know that both the ship and the lake would soon begin to disappear.

Charles declared that he would build his home beside the nearby Old River near the entrance into Lost Lake. I will call the place for my home *The Cove*, he said. Louis made ready to search east of the Trinity River for his ranch land, while Juan and Tall Dan were excited to go back to their homes in Mexico and New Orleans, carrying as much gold as they could on their backs. Lafitte had generously paid them each a hundred gold and silver coins, so each man buried what he could not carry and the four good friends vowed honesty and secrecy to one another until they returned. Then they made a pact that whatever was buried would belong to the others if one of them did not return in three years.

There was no way to carry the remaining treasure with them, so Charles carved the initials, CT, into into a nearby oak tree to mark the spot and they buried the sacks together beside the tree. They swore an oath to each other to take only their own coins and to protect the other's treasure at all costs.

The following morning, the men shook hands and said, "Goodbye." After Juan and Tall Dan had set off on their travels, Louis and Charles unrolled the rugs containing their sacks of treasure from Barataria. They decided to also bury their Barataria treasure on the other side of the tree, after taking as much gold as they needed to travel.

That night Charles finally said, "I want to go home to New Hampshire for a visit. I will come back next year for the rest of my gold and silver. Come with me, Louis. I am sure my family will welcome you like a son." He had come to think of Louis as a little brother rather than a good friend and now hated to leave him behind.

"Merci, my friend, thank you, but I am eager to explore the land east of here and find a good piece for a ranch of my own," replied Louis, eagerly. I will apply for the free Mexican Land Grant available for farmers and ranchers to make the land mine. Then I will come back for my gold so I can build a fine home and buy many cattle. Perhaps I will even have a wife when we meet again next year." He grinned broadly.

Charles understood Louis' need to put down roots and assured him that he also would return in a year, for he liked the Texas coast's warm climate and the lush forests with abundant game. People from the United States were beginning to move to this land and apply to the Mexican Government for free farm and ranch land grants. With the free land, even though Mexico owned Texas, it was a chance for a new life. He believed that someday in the near future Galveston Island would become a busy seaport.

That last night, lying beside the lake under the stars, the two boys, now grown, talked about ways of bringing up the boat's brass cannons and the expensive, heavy, copper sheets that Bos had laid over the deck for extra protection. They felt confident that they would be able to find the *Black Jack* and their buried treasure later with their crude maps.

Chapter 17:

Going Home to New Hampshire~~1820

Charles, now twenty-one and grown, looked forward to making the long trip back to New Hampshire to see his family again. It had been over six years since he had stood on the whaler and watched them wave good-bye to him on the New Hampshire wharf. He had sent several letters but had no way of knowing if they had ever gotten through.

First he applied and received a free land grant of over a thousand acres from the Mexican Government for his Cove homestead. There were no settlers in the area as yet, so he staked out his new land. Then, at last, in the late spring Charles bought a good horse, a new saddle and a rifle for four of his precious doubloons and dug up as many as he could carry in a saddlebag. Then he set out toward his family home a thousand miles away. There were a few roads in 1820, so he traveled mainly by the rivers using a compass. He rode from settlement to settlement, fording streams, and often sleeping under the stars.

Charles' saddlebags were heavy with doubloons and extra clothes but his horse was strong. Sometimes he came upon a farm and was given an evening meal and a bed of hay in the barn. He smiled when he thought of the poor farmer who would find a silver piece of eight gleaming on his front porch the next morning and the mysterious guest gone. The farther east he journeyed, the larger the towns became. Soon he was able to stay in hotels and board his horse in stables. He needed to take only several gold doubloons into a bank for the happily surprised bank president to exchange them for enough money for his trip.

Charles heads Home

After almost four months of travel, in September of 1820, he reached New England, the land of his childhood. Red and yellow leaves of autumn streaked the trees as he neared the town of New Hampton, New Hampshire.

Charles clicked his tongue and flicked the reins of his horse to hasten his pace.

"Come on, boy, we're almost home!" A lump rose in his throat and would not go away.

News had already spread far and wide through the area that the Tilton boy, missing since the spring of 1814, was alive and on his way home.

"Look, that's him! That be the Tilton boy!" an old lady cried and waved her hands.

"I would know him anywhere—looks just like his dad, he does. Hello, Charles!"

"Welcome home, Lad!" called another.

Charles waved and smiled at the town's people, but continued to gallop toward home. He could not stop to visit old friends now.

A tall, slender boy stood waiting at the bend in the town's road. As Charles neared, the boy ran out in front of him waving, causing Charles to rein in his horse. "Charles, it's me, Ethan, your little brother! Welcome back!"

Charles reached down and pulled his brother up onto the horse. "Ethan, I didn't recognize you. Come on, brother, let's go home together!" Charles shouted and grinned as he nudged the horse into a gallop again.

A friend banged on the Tilton Family's door. "A young man is riding into town. I think it be your son. Come quickly!"

Ethan Tilton

Charles's mother, whose face was lined and hair was now streaked with gray from grief for her oldest son, and his father, now using a walking cane, hurried down the cobblestone street as fast as they could. They hardly dared to hope that this was their long-lost son. Indeed, the entire town had come out and lined the street beside the wharf, cheering as though a famous dignitary were riding by. As soon as Charles saw his parents, he jumped down from his horse and gave the reins to Ethan. He began running toward his parents. The couple stood frozen in doubt to the cobblestone street.

"Mother, Father! It's Charles! Don't you know me?" he cried as he neared them. Suddenly Judith and Green Tilton recognized their long lost son, now grown up.

"Charles, is it really thee? Our Charles has finally come home!" They kept repeating as they flung their arms around him, wept with joy and held him tightly. His smallest brothers, Jonah and Matthew, came clamoring up to him and hugged him.

A pretty, dimpled girl shyly handed him a handful of flowers and smiled. Charles looked carefully at her and suddenly realized that it was little Molly, now fifteen years old and beautiful. "Molly, Miriam!" he cried, amazed at how much his sisters had grown up in six years.

A great reunion was held for the boy who was now a young man. The entire town wanted to celebrate the return of one of its own whalers. Women cooked while men carried benches and tables to the Tilton's yard. Flags were hung on the house and soon it was turned into a festive party area. The next day people began to arrive. Old friends came, eager to hear Charles' story and shake his hand. His other brothers and sisters, now grown and married, came in wagons and on horseback to see their brother.

Charles was visiting a neighbor when he felt a hand on his shoulder. Turning around, he looked into the kindly, sea-worn face. He thought he recognized the old man but couldn't quite place him. "Charles Tilton, I'd know you anywhere," he said. Realizing that the young man before him did not know who he was, he added, "'Tis Captain Thatcher, laddie. Do you not recognize me?"

Charles was so shocked that he dropped his mug of cider on the ground as he grabbed the captain's shoulders. "Can it be?" he cried. "Captain, you're alive! How I prayed you and the other men would live."

"Aye, and fit as a fiddle," the captain replied, laughing. Before Charles could ask, he explained that after floating for two days without food or water, a passing whaler had spotted the three small boats and picked up the men. "We thought the pirates had killed you too, yet here we be, both alive and well! God has been kind to us, indeed."

Charles smiled and nodded. A great weight seemed to lift off his shoulders. "And what of Corky?"

"He would be here if he could, but he and his family now live in Boston," the captain added. "I will write him straightaway and let him know that you are alive."

Finally in the evening, the happy well wishers went back to their homes, leaving Charles to visit his big family. Though not surprised, they were sorry to learn that none of his letters had ever reached them.

Charles' mother took him by the hand and led him to the front parlor window that faced the ocean. She pointed to a little hurricane lamp glowing on the windowsill and blew it out. At last, her son who was lost was home from the sea. "I always prayed ye might be alive, though everyone else told me differently. My prayers have been answered. Thee is finally home," she said softly. She held Charles' face in her wrinkled hands and wept again with happiness.

"There now, Mother. See, I am still wearing the cross you gave me. I am fine and have many adventures to tell you about," Charles replied.

Green Tilton Open the Saddlebag

Then he surprised his family by emptying the large saddlebag of gold coins onto the table. "Take it all and use it to make your lives easier." Seeing his father's worried glance, he said, "I earned it all honestly, working for a just and generous man, whom many people thought of as an evil pirate though I knew his kinder side, a privateer with permission and a contract from the United States Government to rid the Gulf of the Spanish Galleons. The government allowed us to keep the spoils and I still have plenty for myself." The family could not believe that he had brought such a gift and they stared in amazement at the glittering pile, for they had never even held a gold piece.

He stayed through the fall and winter in New Hampton, but, all the while, he felt the tug of his new Texas land. He told all of his family his capture by Rooster and Groggins and about Jean Lafitte's kindness and the years of sailing with the privateer. He also told them about Texas' warm weather, free land grants from Mexico, the beautiful beaches, fertile soil and the abundance of water, game, and forests. He encouraged his brothers to bring their families and move with him to Texas. The promise of free land interested them and several expressed a desire to join him in a year or two.

Charles' parents were excited that he now owned land and could make a good living for himself. New railroads lines were being built every day and he expected one to soon open to New Orleans. He was able and willing to pay for their trip to come by locomotive to see him. Charles assured his parents that he would come meet them there and sail them to his home for a long visit.

The evening before Charles left New Hampshire, Green stood at the table and raised his glass to toast his oldest son. Slowly, he cleared his throat and his voice cracked when he spoke, just as it did when he said *good-bye* to his young boy six years ago.

"Son, we are forever grateful for your great generosity. It will be used wisely by all of us. However, as much as we thank you for this gift of prosperity, we want you to know that **you** are the best gift the Lord has ever given us." Tears of love filled the eyes of Charles' parents and of all his brothers and sisters as he smiled humbly. The boy who, so long ago, had been kidnapped by pirates at sea had come home again, this time as a successful young man.

Chapter 18:

Mystery of the Sunken Pirate Ship

Going Home to Texas--1821

When spring came, Charles knew it was time for him to leave New Hampshire and return to his land. He reminded his parents and brothers and sisters again that he would pay their way to come for a visit, as soon as the new railroad line came through. Then he bid his family farewell for the second time in his life.

Returning to his Cove homestead, Charles went to the carved oak tree on the bank of Lost Lake and dug up some of his Barataria treasure, being careful not to disturb his friends' sacks that still lay buried. Then, he headed to Galveston, now a busy, growing seaport. Once there, he used more of his doubloons to purchase a ninety-ton schooner from an old man whom he recognized from their days with Lafitte. The ship was not new, but the wood and the sails were sound, the barnacles had been scraped off the sides and it was freshly painted blue. Charles paid the old seaman with doubloons and the two men grinned and winked as they shook hands, both remembering where the gold had come from. Charles loved the sea and joked that he must have salt water in his blood. He named the large, double-masted schooner *Black Jack II*.

The next morning, as the warm sun rose in a lemon-haze sky, Charles watched the seagulls dip their bills into the water for a small fish then sail up into the sky. As he sailed out into Galveston Bay, he smiled because he felt so at peace on the sea and he knew his destiny would always be joined to it. He crossed the bay and sailed up the Trinity River and into Old River to the calm, wooded inlet he called *The Cove*. Here, Charles anchored his boat and stepped onto his land. He was finally home.

*****

Charles and Annie

Evelyn Gill Hilton

Charles Gets Married

Charles built a home and a pier there on the bank of Old River. Later, he met a Spirited, dark-haired girl named Annie Barber in the nearby settlement of Barber's Hill. After courting the pretty, outspoken young lady, she agreed to marry him and he brought her to his Cove homestead to live. The next year, a little baby boy was born to the happy couple and they named him Benjamin. Over the years, they had a big family of nine children. The last one, Laura, was seventeen years younger than Ben, but they were always close because both of them shared their father's great love of the sea. However, that is another story for another time and is the second book in this series.

Charles farmed and ranched and, when other homesteaders moved into the area, he began his ship hauling business between the Old River and Trinity River settlements and the Galveston seaport. Texas was still a part of Mexico and a frontier. There were no good roads for farmers to move their produce but Charles could easily haul them on his boat. He transported rice from their rice fields, vegetables from their gardens, and even cattle to Galveston to sell to ship merchants and brought back much-needed goods, money and tools for them. Together, he and Annie worked hard and made a good life for themselves and their children. Charles became a well-known friend and neighbor to the settlers who continued to move to the Texas Coast and to Galveston.

Charles' Cove Home

The Greatest Treasures

Charles still hoped to someday bring up the *Black Jack's* treasures, but something happened that no one could have foretold. The big, heavy ship slowly began to sink into the lake's soft mud bottom and silt from Old River gradually filled in the entrance to the lake, hiding the pirate schooner deep beneath its surface.

Charles Louis Cronea, his good friend, also retrieved his share of the doubloons they had buried beside Lost Lake. In the following years, he would drive his wagon or ride his horse from his ranch from time to time for a visit. They would go out to the banks of Lost Lake to see once again where the *Black Jack* lay buried. Charles would also visit Louis and his family at his ranch close to the present-day town of Sabine Pass, Texas near the Gulf. Over the years, Lost Lake dried up and became a grassy field with grazing cattle. The mast that had served as a great diving place in the lake for Charles and Annie's children finally disappeared, as did the oak tree with its carved initials.

"I think the old *Black Jack* and its treasure are forever lost," Charles said sadly to his friend.

"Oui, mon ami, but we will always have our friendship and rich memories and those are far greater than any treasure," Louis answered in his French accent as he patted Charles' shoulder. Charles hardily agreed, for the two had shared many, many priceless adventures.

EPILOGUE:

Through the Years

Many Years Later....

Charles' daughter, Ann, gave her grandson, Arnold, a piece of land for a home beside the Lost Lake field. One day, an old man rode up to his house on a burro. Unable to speak much English, the man patted his chest and said, "Juan," then pointed in the direction of Mexico and added, "Juarez," a city just over the Texas border. He pulled a piece of old, animal skin out, unrolled it and held it out for them to see. Arnold was stunned to see that burned into the wrinkled leather was a crude map of Old River and Lost Lake. There was an X and a picture of a ship in the middle of the lake. He suddenly he understood the reason for Juan Martinez's long journey.

The old man saw Arnold's astonishment and said, "Mi Grandpapa amigo de Senior Tilton." Arnold understood enough Spanish to know that Juan was telling him that his Grandfather was Charles' friend and had helped sail the pirate schooner into Lost Lake in 1820. Arnold had often heard family stories about the sinking of the ship and the maps on animal skins, but he had never seen one of them.

Arnold invited the old man to stay for dinner and, afterward, took him out to see the grassy field and grazing cattle and pointed down to the ground. He scooped up some dirt with his hand to show the old man where the schooner lay buried. "Here, Aqui," he said. Later, Arnold told the family that the old man stood on the site and wept. It seemed as though his dream had died. Sadly, he got back on his burro and rode off in the direction of Mexico.

Charles Tilton's Legacy

In fact, no one has ever been able to dig up the schooner, although two excavating companies have tried. The mast is gone, the maps are long gone, the tree bearing the initials and even the lake are gone. It is a fact however, documented in history books, that Jean Lafitte had brass cannons and a thick, solid, copper deck on this seventy-five ton schooner, the *Black Jack*. The old ship, deep beneath the field of Lost Lake, could be worth millions, although it may remain a mystery forever. But Charles Tilton's legacy as a Texas pioneer lives on.

Charles Tilton, the brave, young boy who had been captured by rogue pirates and then became a buccaneer with the famous Jean Lafitte, grew up to become a staunch, enduring citizen. Like so many other pioneers, he played a vital part in settling our state and shaping our nation. Besides being a hard worker and a good father, he lived his faith and beliefs by joining a church and becoming an elder in it, as well as a highly respected citizen who served his community. We are indebted to him and all of the other courageous, sturdy pioneers like him who played an important role in forming our country's great history.

Fighting for Texas' Independence

In March of 1836, the Texians (as Texans were called when Texas belonged to Mexico) declared independence from Mexico. Mexico sent General Santa Anna and his army of two thousand soldiers marching across Texas to stamp out the "little rebellion."

At a small, adobe mission called *The Alamo,* in the village of San Antonio, one hundred eighty-nine determined men, led by Colonel William B. Travis and Jim Bowie, fought bravely for the right to be free against the huge Mexican army. Santa Anna and his soldiers overran the mission walls and ended the Texians' battle for freedom at the Alamo by putting every man there to death. However, they could not stamp out the Texians' will to be free.

When Charles and Annie heard about the Alamo, they were as shocked and furious as every other Texian. Charles decided to join General Sam Houston's army. He enlisted and was put in charge of Houston's personal baggage wagon as the army moved.

On April 21, 1836, Santa Anna and his army made camp beside the San Jacinto River (near present-day Houston). Sam Houston's Texian scouts soon located them and he formed a daring plan. Houston knew the army had a custom of taking a siesta, or nap, every day and would never expect a bold attack from the small Texian army, so Houston divided his army into two groups. He ordered his first group of soldiers to crawl quietly through the weeds to within a rock's throw of the Mexican camp, while the second group of horsemen and wagoneers, which included Charles, hid themselves in a nearby grove of oak trees.

As soon as Houston gave the order, the men on foot jumped up and ran toward the camp, whooping and firing their rifles. Immediately, the second group galloped in and they all shouted over and over, "Remember the Alamo! Remember the Alamo!" This created great panic among Santa Anna's men, who were awakened and taken completely by surprise. Before the Mexican soldiers could pull their boots on, the *Battle of San Jacinto* was over and Santa Anna was captured. At last, the Texians were free from Mexico and the Republic of Texas was born!

General Houston gave each soldier three hundred and twenty acres of homestead land as payment for their service. Charles chose land along Old River adjoining the land he already farmed. Owning so much land was a dream-come-true for Charles and Annie.

Living in a Free Republic in 1836

As Charles and Annie's children grew up, they often swam in nearby Lost Lake and dove off the crow's nest atop the sunken *Black Jack's* mast, but every year, it dropped a little more as the ship sank deeper and deeper into mud. All of the boys and the youngest girl, brave little Laura, could dive from the crow's nest deep into the water and swim down to touch the thick copper plating that Lafitte had put over the ship's deck long ago.

Charles had a special place in his heart for his youngest child, daring Laura. While her sisters wanted to help their mother cook and sew, she begged her father and older brother, Ben, to teach her how to steer the schooner and raise the sails. Charles often commented that if Laura had been a boy, she would have surely been a sailor.

"No, Father, I would be a buccaneer just like you and Jean Lafitte!" tomboy Laura's green eyes would flash as she answered. (You can Read Laura and Ben's story in Book II of this series.)

Living in the State of Texas

It was 1845 and Texas was still mostly frontier land being settled by sturdy pioneers. They voted to join the United States and entered the Union as the twenty-eighth state. Everyone in Texas celebrated their new statehood in the United States of America!

Charles and Annie continued living in their Old River home, running their hauling business to Galveston and raising their children. Eventually the children grew up, married and had many children of their own. Charles' grandchildren always enjoyed listening to his tales about his childhood in New Hampshire and his exciting buccaneer days with the famous Jean Lafitte.

He was liked far and wide by everyone around for his honesty and friendliness and he never wished that his life had taken a different turn. Charles Tilton had traveled each new path in life that opened before him with courage and faith and had done his best. That was the way of a good pioneer.

Note From the Author:

Today, the Tilton Cemetary has an official Texas Historical Marker in honor of Charles Tilton. It is in the Cove community beside Old River, which runs into the Trinity and is near present day Baytown, Texas.

Kidnapped by Pirates is the first book of my *Texas Trails' Young Heroes Series*. Thank you for reading this book about my great-great grandfather and his friend, Jean Lafitte. I hope you enjoyed it and learned more about the exciting history of our great state and nation.

The second book of the series is about Charles Tilton's daughter, Laura, who went through the Great Galveston Hurricane of 1900 with her brother, Ben. It is entitled, Annabelle and the Great Galveston Hurricane and is based on the life of my great grandmother, Laura Tilton.

The Texas Trails Series' third book is entitled Old 300 Wagon Train Kids and is based on the true story of Amy White and her seven children. A recent widow, she came as the only lone woman bringing her unique sons and daughters, to the wild Texas frontier with Stephen F. Austin's group of 300 settlers.

If you wish to order one of my books, please go to www.texastrails.com. Happy Reading!"

Sincerely,

Evelyn Gill Hilton

Made in the ŪSA
Lexington, KY
12 December 2015